Also by Jaron Lee Knuth

The Superhumans
Fixing Sam

AFTER LIFE

by Jaron Lee Knuth

This is a work of fiction. Names, characters, places, and incidents are either the product of the author's imagination or are used fictitiously. Any resemblance to actual persons, living or dead, events, or locales is entirely coincidental.

Copyright © 2009 by Jaron Lee Knuth

Fourth Edition

This book is licensed under Creative Commons Attribution-Noncommercial-Share Alike 3.0 United States

For Marnie

Day 1

9:54 am

Alex pulled aside the thin, stained curtains and peered out the frosted glass of his kitchen window. The polluted snow that floated down slowly from the gray sky collected near the bottom. People outside ran for cover, the lucky ones pulled their hoods over their heads and they zipped up the front of their jackets even tighter, securing their winter armor.

The meteorologist had missed another storm, but no one could blame him anymore. A storm like that was expected in January, not the middle of May. Mother Nature had become an unpredictable bitch and that day Minneapolis was her bedpan.

As the young, out-of-shape man turned away from the window he caught a glimpse of his neighbor, Mr. Peterson, chipping ice from the windshield of his car parked on the street. For some reason Mr. Peterson insisted on parking there instead of his allocated parking spot in the back of the building. Alex stopped and he watched the overweight man smash away at the frozen sheet that encompassed the entire vehicle. He smiled, feeling a twinge

AFTER LIFE

of retribution as he watched his most rage-fueled neighbor grow more and more irate with his own luck.

Not only was it a reminder of how grateful he was to have the day off from work, but Alex despised his neighbor. Mr. Peterson was a poster child for Alex's list of pet peeves. The man's temper was out of control, and Alex was forced to listen to him scream at his teenage daughter every night. When Alex had the misfortune of running into his neighbor outside the apartment building, Mr. Peterson always insisted on telling Alex a racist, sexist, or otherwise socially ignorant "joke." Couple these bad personality traits with his unending consumption of alcohol and the man became Alex's arch enemy.

Not that Alex would ever be brave enough to confront him.

Alex let his body crumple onto his couch, letting out an exhausted sigh as he sunk into the permanent crease that had formed from his days of occupation. He felt no physical exhaustion, but his mind was feeling weak. Seeing the man beat down by nature was satisfying, but only served to remind Alex of his own social impotence. His own fear made him a pacifist. His anti-social behavior was beginning to feel more like agoraphobia.

Alex felt the emptiness of his apartment creep around him, echoing in its hollowness. The shelves of action figures, collection of movie replica swords, and pile of classic video game consoles did nothing to fill his metaphorical void. The rumble of his neighbor Denny stomping across the floor, and the laughter of Denny's girlfriend were the only noises in the apartment. Her cackles were caused by what Alex would only surmise was pointless, mediocre humor.

His mind began filing through images of his friends one by one. He thought of those friends he barely talked to and those that had drifted away. The friends no longer interested in his dead-end life. The friends that had become married. The friends with children. The friends who had a better time with a bottle of liquor than with him. He pictured his co-workers. The people like him who turned to a job at Wal-Mart instead of college. They were, for the most part, good people, yet Alex found boredom in all of them. The people outside his apartment had become distant strangers from a foreign land, speaking in a language he didn't understand and holding to cultural traditions that seemed disgusting and strange.

As the pictures of these people flipped through his head, his eyes drifted toward his laptop. The screen was only open half an inch, but the it lit the keys below it. He left it that way on the coffee table so the machine wouldn't shut down and cancel his bit torrent program. The illegally downloaded movies and music took his mind off the slowly creeping hours that awaited the rest of the day, but the true draw of the computer's glow was the flashing red light on the corner of the screen. The light that let him know someone was trying to start an instant message conversation.

Morgan.

It had to be her.

Alex snatched the computer off the table, wondering how long he had ignored it for, worrying she would cancel the call before he responded. The icon still flashed, asking him if he wanted to respond with chat, or voice. His fingers slid across the touch pad, too nervous for accuracy. He consciously slowed his hand downand he managed to click on the phone icon.

"Hello?" Alex's voice was scratchy, gurgling phlegm into the word. He realized how long it had been since he had spoken and cleared his throat. "Hello? Can you hear me?"

"Yes? Can you hear me?" The voice was breathy, sultry in the most subtle way possible, even through the distorted computer speakers.

AFTER LIFE

"Yes!" He took a deep breath, suddenly embarrassed by his excitement, before asking, "How's it going?"

"Good, good. I'm just taking a break from work." Morgan created her own online comic. Her site had begun reaching some bigger numbers and advertisers had taken notice. She was finally able to relax when it came to paying the bills and this afforded her a much more tranquil attitude overall, a sharp contrast from the neurotic worrier Alex had grown to adore. But her new nonchalant lifestyle made Alex feel uneasy around her. Almost as if she was leaving him behind on a lower level of maturity.

"What were you working on?" His voice trembled between sincere interest and passive small talk.

Whenever he talked to her he had to re-analyze what "angle" to take with her. He sometimes thought a passive attitude would push her to become more pro-active when it came to hanging out, or just finding time to talk to him. It seemed the more he pulled away, the closer she stepped in. That made him feel wanted, which was something his diet severely lacked.

While that felt selfishly good, his true feelings always came out. He was a horrible liar and even worse at playing any kind of social "game." He wanted to be there for her in every capacity. He yearned to know everything about her because he truly found her *that* interesting. So he always leapt to her attention, and begged for the same affection in return.

"I'm just trying to finish today's strip." Morgan's voice sounded tired. Bored.

"What's wrong?"

She sighed loudly, pausing for a dramatically long moment before answering, "Nothing, really. Just bored with... everything."

"Everything?" He knew she was being vague, but wouldn't let her get away with it. He wanted to show his interest, so he dug deeper. "Are you just bored with your comic?"

"Yes," she said. "And life in general."

"Oh come on." He tried to keep his tone light hearted. He didn't want her to talk herself into her own depression. "You can't mean that. What's at the top of your list?"

She sighed again, struggling to get her thoughts out. Finally she said, "My list of things I'm bored with? I don't know. I read a bad review of my comic this morning and I know, I know. It was just some dumbass with a blog, but-"

"What did they say?"

"It doesn't even matter. It's just..."

The silence lingered.

"What is it, Morgan?"

"Can you meet me for coffee or something? I seriously can't work today. I need to smoke like a million cigarettes."

Alex cringed. She knew he hated her smoking. He had tried smoking once and never smoked again. His mind brought up memories of cigarettes mixed with her perfume, but he pushed the thought away.

"Of course. Where do you want to go?"

"Somewhere war. This weather is fucked up. Are people ever going to realize we are totally fucking the environment up?" Morgan cursed freely when she was feeling confident, or trying to give the impression of confidence.

"We need to go outside the city limits if you want to smoke." He tried his hardest to control his tone. He truly didn't want her to feel guilty for smoking. It wasn't his place.

She made a noise of agreement before saying, "I can come pick you up if you want."

Alex felt emasculated for a fraction of a second before he remembered Mr. Peterson. The thought of that man's frustration allowed Alex to remember that he liked not owning a car.

"Yeah, sure." Alex tempered his excitement. He hadn't seen Morgan in over a month and the last meeting was only a brief encounter. Not to mention she was always with her fiancé. He couldn't wait to see her. Seeing her alone was almost too good to be true. He considered her, in some strange way, to be his best friend, even though they barely spoke anymore.

"Okay, um..." She paused, as if considering something silently. "I need to do a few things around the house and then I'll be over."

For some reason, her nonchalant attitude bothered him, but he didn't let it show. "Cool. Just honk twice when you're in the parking lot. That way you don't have to get out in this snow."

She ended the conversation simply. "Okay, I'll see you in a bit."

The icon on the screen grayed out with the message, "Call disconnected. Do you want to re-connect?" He clicked the *NO* button and then he checked his downloads. Most of them had completed overnight. He left his computer on out of courtesy to all the people now downloading the files from him.

In the bathroom he stared at himself in the mirror. He knew he had to shave, but couldn't decide what he should do with the 3 weeks of growth. He knew Morgan liked facial hair, but wasn't sure what looked good on him. After trimming his beard into a mustache and goatee, he then realized he hated the mustache so he shaved the mustache and left just a goatee. Alex finally just shaved his entire face clean.

Maybe I'll seem more kissable, he caught himself thinking as he ran his fingers over his smooth cheeks. He rolled his eyes at himself, feeling slightly pathetic for still having thoughts like that.

He had, in the past, hoped there was a chance for something beyond friendship with Morgan. They had been friends ever since they tried dating in the seventh grade. A single night at a birthday party. It was the same night they both tried smoking for the first time. After pretending they both enjoyed the cigarette, he had kissed Morgan. They made out for hours underneath a streetlight on the road in front of the party, stopping only to nervously smoke more cigarettes. After the seventh or eighth cigarette, while Alex's tongue was exploring Morgan's mouth and ignoring the pain from her braces, his hand began to reach up her shirt. Just as he it past he navel his stomach began to rumble uncomfortably. The cigarettes had made his head woozy and now his stomach was reacting.

Being a pre-pubescent boy, at first he ignored the pain, concentrating instead upon his fingers and their ever so slow march up Morgan's belly. But, soon it became too much for him to ignore. His stomach groaned loudly and they both pulled away from each other in shock.

It was right at that moment that a crowd of kids started making noises. A crowd of kids who had gathered behind the tree to watch the two of them kiss. With hoots, hollers, and everyone making kissing noises, the kids poured out from the shadows.

Something gripped Alex's stomach, twisting all of the birthday Cake and Mountain Dew he had ingested through the night. His eyes went white as his head lurched forward. He released the contents of his stomach, spraying the liquid ooze from his mouth. He had aimed away from Morgan, but the splatter effect worked against him, flinging his dinner all over her feet and legs. He fell to his knees in pain, releasing a second load of fluid onto the pavement.

His eyes were blurred with tears, but he heard the laughter. The group of kids began mocking Morgan relentlessly. It was his faux pas, but their minds had found another conclusion.

AFTER LIFE

"Morgan metal mouth ain't so cute! If you kiss her, she'll make you puke!"

The chant didn't even rhyme well, but it was easy to remember and remember they did. The story lingered for years. Alex was mocked for kissing poor "Morgan metal mouth", but it was infrequent and easy to dodge. She was the real victim of the night.

One month later he gave her a mix CD he had burned for her. In black magic marker were the words: "I'm sorry" written over and over again as many times as he could fit. It was filled with the darkest emo-rock he could find.

She called him a few days later, and after that they talked on the phone nearly every night of high school. They foolishly agreed that they should just be friends, but it didn't take long for Alex to develop real feelings for her. Deep rooted feelings that went beyond the temptation of just putting his hand up her shirt.

Although that feeling was still there, too.

She dated other men, and she always called Alex when it didn't work out. They talked about love, dating, and sex. They found that they agreed on almost everything. They could talk for hours about the simplest of subjects and analytically tear them down. They laughed at dark humor and openly cried with each other. He introduced her to comics and she drew him notebooks full of pictures.

But they never touched the subject of dating each other. When high school ended and college started, Alex began rejecting his own feelings. His hope began to fail.

And then Morgan got engaged.

Her fiancé, Christopher, was nice enough. While she was going to school for web design, he was studying Drama. He loved to talk about movies, was intelligent, attractive, and got along with everyone.

He was the loss of hope for Alex.

Alex never spoke a word of discouragement. He used morals to justify why he felt he should respect both of their decisions to marry. The truth was he had lost any self-esteem that would have made him feel worthy of her. He had no money to offer her, and Christopher's family was beyond rich. He wasn't popular, nor did he get good grades. He was depressed more often than not and found himself complaining about life more than enjoying it.

Their friendship became random emails and the occasional mutual acquaintance's party. He always smiled and nodded at Christopher's self-righteous rants on the genius of Tim Burton. He watched in silent protest as Christopher had "private rehearsals" with every attractive cast member of his student films. Yet, Morgan appeared happy. She talked of the beauty of "open relationships," and the maturity and honesty it took to accept each other as people who make mistakes. Infidelity had become "the adult thing to do."

It only served to convince Alex that Morgan was wrong for him. He told himself that she had grown incompatible with him. He was loyal if nothing else and considered it a trait he would require in a partner. He told himself she had changed too much to make him happy.

He also thought he had only himself to blame for his sadness, and did so daily.

As impossible as his romantic delusions were now, he still found himself worrying if he put on too much cologne before she picked him up. He decided he had and he flapped the hooded sweatshirt in front of him, hoping to air it out.

While he waved the sweatshirt around his apartment he suddenly heard the double honk from the parking lot and ran to the window. Morgan's tiny, blue Volkswagen sat in the parking lot with its wipers furiously trying to keep the huge flakes of snow off the windshield.

Alex put on his faded gray shirt on and grabbed his black pea coat. He slipped his boots on in the hallway while he locked his door. He walked down the back stairwell and tugged an old knit cap down over his head. He then pulled the hood of his sweatshirt over that before stepping out into the blizzard.

Keeping his head down and his face out of the falling flakes, Alex ran to the passenger side door of Morgan's car, high stepping through the drifting snow. He grabbed for the latch and found the door locked. Morgan laughed inside the car and leaned over, popping the lock up with the tips of her fingers.

As he burst into the car trying to escape the weather, Morgan shouted, "Hey!" and pointed angrily at his boots. "I don't want that shit in my car!"

Alex looked down at his boots and saw the ugly snow all over them. He smiled and banged his feet together outside her perfectly maintained car, knocking the clumps of wet, dirty mud onto the ground.

"Hi," he finally said with a smile. Smoke from Morgan's cigarette mingled with the scent of a vanilla air freshener. "How's it going?"

Morgan shrugged her shoulders. Her short curly hair hung in a crazy frizz around her thick black rimmed glasses. She raised one eyebrow in a frustrated contemplation and answered all in one breath, "Some dude just randomly ran out in front of my car on the way here and I almost killed him. It's snowing in May. My fiancé left for California today, and some douche-bag on the Internet thinks my comic is 'a feminist, man hating diatribe blaming western culture and the current presidential administration for every misogynistic oversight ever made by mankind.' Can you believe that? Misogynistic oversight? What the fuck does that even mean?"

"Christopher went to California?" Alex blurted the question out, ignoring any other words she may have said.

Morgan laughed as she blew out smoke from her mouth. Her lips were plush and slightly chapped. "Yeah, his agent got him an audition for a really good role."

"I thought he was going to do that play? The one about the homosexual trees?" Alex was scared of the answer.
The play was the only thing keeping them in Minnesota now that Christopher had graduated. He talked all the time about how he couldn't decide between Hollywood and New York. The Minneapolis theater scene wasn't even an option for the movie obsessed actor. Fame was what he craved.
Alex disallowed his mind from lingering on the idea of losing one of his last friends.
"He's still going to do the play. Filming wouldn't begin until next January, so it's perfect for him."
She spun her tires a bit and Alex secretly hoped he wouldn't have to get out into the snow and push. Her tires finally gripped hard and the car lurched forward. She didn't bother trying to stop before leaving the parking lot and pulled directly into traffic. The back end of the car slid a little farther than she intended, but she righted herself and started their journey out of town.
"What is he auditioning for?" Alex asked, hoping he could learn more about the trip and their plans without sounding like he was snooping.
"Some Spielberg alien movie. I don't remember the name. The Blue Light? The Blue Night? Something." She waved her cigarette into the air, acting as if it wasn't that important. "He's auditioning for the scientist who figures out that the aliens are here to help, and he tries to talk the president out of nuking them."
"That doesn't sound very original."
"Whatever. It's Spielberg so it's good for his career, for sure." She smushed her cigarette butt into the ashtray as they pulled onto the interstate on-ramp.
"So like, if he gets the part are you guys moving?" Alex glanced at her out of the corner of his eye, trying not to appear desperate for an answer.

AFTER LIFE

She just shrugged her shoulders again and said, "I'm not sure."

Her attitude was infuriating to him some times.

She's acting like it's no big deal, he thought. *Did she really care so little about me? Did it really not bother her to move away from me?*

He looked out the window, watching the traffic build up as they merged onto I-94 and she headed out of Minneapolis. Giant SUV's, pick-up trucks, and eighteen-wheelers boxed them in on all sides and the smell of exhaust started leaking through the tiny car's heater.

"Oh man, that's so obnoxious." Morgan reached over and turned off the fan in the heater, trying to cut down the smell. She immediately pulled out another cigarette and lit it.

Alex decided to change the subject back to what he thought Morgan really wanted to talk about. "You aren't actually letting this blogger get to you, are you?"

"No," she said. "I mean, I don't know."

"Morgan! Come on. You get tons of fan mail every day. You can't let some kid with a blog affect your-"

"No, no." She cut him off, waving the hand with the cigarette casually toward him. "I know. I mean, I just needed to get out of the house. Too much crap all at once, ya know?"

"Okay. Just remember how many people love your work."

With no response to his statement, Morgan asked, "How about that diner in Stillwater? You can still smoke there, right?" Without waiting for an answer, Morgan merged into the exit lane.

As soon as she pulled out from behind the large semi-truck in front of them, she let out a scream, that caused Alex to jolt his head forward and look out the windshield.

In the middle of the far right lane, stood a man dragging his feet through the shin deep snow.

Morgan jerked her arm to the side, spinning the steering wheel toward Alex. The car turned sideways, but it continued to slide forward, directly at the man. Alex braced himself against the dashboard and Morgan continued screaming.

"Shit, shit, shit!" Morgan's words stumbled out of her mouth until she screamed at the top of her lungs, "Dude, look out!"

The car kept sliding down the highway sideways, but the man made no motion to move out of the way. He kept walking slowly, dragging one of his legs behind him as if it were broken.

At the last second the car's tires gripped the pavement and the small Volkswagen lurched to the side of the road. Its rear bumper just missed the man in the road. Alex looked out the back window and saw the man didn't even flinch as they zoomed past him.

Morgan twirled the wheel around, directing the car back at the road so they didn't continue into the snow bank. She managed to wrestle the car into control and it slowed at the stop sign at the bottom of the exit ramp.

"Oh my god," Morgan said, resting her head on the steering wheel when the car completely stopped.

Alex reached over and almost placed his hand on her back, but pulled it back. "It's okay, Morgan. It's okay. You did good. You did really good." He said these meaningless words of comfort, even though Morgan would require none. His tongue felt swollen and his brain was flush with adrenalin. He could barely think straight.

"What is with people today? I almost hit a guy on the way to pick you up and then this. What is wrong with people today? Was that frickin' guy homeless?" She gasped. Alex could see her cheeks flush red with anger. She turned her head toward him. "What was he doing? He wasn't even wearing a coat! I almost killed him! Alex, I almost killed him! *Unnhh!*" Morgan shook her hands out in front of her as

AFTER LIFE

if she was casting water off her skin and pulled her hair back behind her ears. "Now I really need to smoke."

She pulled out from the stop sign and headed toward the town of Stillwater. It was there that a diner supplied coffee and greasy breakfasts for weary travelers. Alex looked down the road, in the opposite direction of Stillwater. There amongst the falling snow three men were wrestling another man to the ground in the middle of the street.

Alex was about to say something, but the car sped away, and soon he couldn't even see the men in the blizzard. Morgan turned on the stereo and the car was filled with one of his favorite songs. This was enough to make him forget about what he saw and he began singing the familiar lyrics.

Day 1

11:08 am

Morgan lit her third cigarette since they had sat down on the red, cracked leather booth. She took a long, deep drag off of the smoke as she smiled at the waitress who was refilling her cup. Outside the window the snow began to let up, but the wind continued blowing it around, causing very low visibility. Many of the customers "ooh-ed" and "aah-ed" as the cars and trucks went sliding through the stoplight in front of the Diner parking lot, barely missing each other. The anticipation for a crash was thick in the air.

"Well *this* is morbid," Alex said, sipping his vanilla shake. He hated the bitterness of coffee. He also liked the fact that he saw just a hint of jealousy in Morgan's eyes when his giant shake came for him, and she got her tiny cup of tar.

"We should be in t-shirts right now," Morgan said, looking out the window longingly. "What the hell did we do to this planet?"

AFTER LIFE

Alex smiled. "We made a lot of money raping the earth. That's what we did."

Morgan, sensing his sarcasm, rolled her eyes. She snatched the cherry off the top of his whip cream and popped it in her mouth.

"Yum," she said, staring directly at him as she slowly chewed the red fruit.

Alex grew uncomfortable with even the slight flirtation and he instead looked at the small TV hanging over the counter. The volume was muted and they had the closed captioning turned on, but on the screen were images of the freak snow storm all over the M,idwest.

Morgan took a sip of coffee and her mouth hung open for a few seconds before she spoke, as if she needed to push past her own thoughts. "Alex, do you think Christopher was a good choice for me?" Even she was taken aback by the randomness of her question, but she had no idea how to segway into the topic. "Do you think he *is* a good choice for me?" Morgan's voice trembled and she took another drag off her cigarette.

She hated asking questions like that. She hated exposing any vulnerability. Her father taught her at an early age that exposing things like that was a sign of weakness. She always suspected this was a lesson he planned to teach the son he never had. Regardless, he had toughened her up more than most girls she knew. In fact, throughout her life, when she saw other girls break down and cry over simple things, or drag out their problems in overly dramatic public situations, she cringed. She saw her own weak self reflected in these moments.

Alex saw things differently. He saw that exposing herself to pain was her true power. Holding a balance between her strength and weakness was the true art. This complexity is what enthralled Alex. Her ever-changing, ever-evolving state of mind is what made her transcend the other people who never grew past one-dimensional parodies of themselves. Her ability to constantly grow and adapt to everything life threw at her. This escaped her personal view of herself. She was the strongest person he knew, yet she refused to see it.

"Alex, are you listening?"

Alex kept looking at the TV, only half aware she was talking. "Morgan," he pointed at the TV, "look at that guy."

Morgan looked over at the TV, ready to yell at Alex for interrupting, but saw a man slowly dragging his feet through the snow, his jaw hanging slightly askew. He wasn't wearing a coat, or hat, or any winter apparel. In fact his clothes looked shredded and torn. Alex got up from his seat and stepped closer so he could read the small print at the bottom of the screen.

"They're saying it's a massive flu epidemic that's causing people to act like that. Wandering around outside no matter what the temperature is. They aren't responding to anyone."

"Just like the guy on the road," Morgan said. She stood up and started reading the scrolling words at the bottom of the screen with Alex.

The words crawled across the screen slowly, revealing their information inch by inch as the videos continued to play.

Outbreaks of the deadly flu have been confirmed nationwide. New reports suggest outbreaks in Europe and Japan

Officials say people suffering from the flu virus have appeared unresponsive and even hostile

The CDC issued a statement calling the speed of the outbreak "unprecedented"

AFTER LIFE

"Oh man, I totally don't want to get sick," Alex said, sitting back down in the booth.

Morgan sat back down and put her cigarette out in the ash tray. She sipped her coffee and shivered as the warm liquid rolled down her throat. She looked across the table at Alex and watched him slurp up the last of his shake.

He looked innocent to her at that moment, like there was nothing else going through his head other than the sweet flavor of vanilla. His normal look of worry and concern was gone, if only for the briefest of seconds. She pushed her glasses up the bridge of her nose and opened her mouth into a tiny smile.

"Look at that guy! He must be sick." A trucker was shouting and pointing out the window.

Everyone looked out through the blowing flakes and saw a man wearing a suit crossing the intersection that all of the cars were sliding through. Instead of taking steps the man lurched forward, thrusting his shoulder to give his body momentum. His feet dragged across the ground and he looked as if he might topple over at any minute. He slowly made his way toward the Diner.

"Someone should help him," one of the waitresses said, passively pleading with the customers.

"Guy is gonna get hit," a trucker mumbled, huffing his breath under his mustache.

The group gasped in unison when a pickup truck sped toward the intersection and locked its breaks. The truck honked its horn as it started spinning out of control, crashing into the man and sending him flying into the diner parking-lot. His body slammed into the side of a semi-trailer flopped on to the ground, leaving a splatter of blood stamped on the trailer where his head had landed. Everyone stood frozen in shock at what they had witnessed. The pickup truck continued to spin and came to a stop nearly a block away. The man's body lay on the ground, still as death.

And then he moved.

Slowly, the man in the suit lifted his arms and pushed against the ground, lifting his body. He gradually pulled his legs underneath, leaning against the semi-truck cab for assistance. Blood poured from his torn open neck with a rhythmic gushing and his head bobbed side to side. Lifeless eyes stared into the diner, and his arms lifted away from his stained suit, which by all accounts was very expensive and nice at one time. His arms reached out toward the window that all the customers were staring out of.

The waitresses screamed. The truckers cursed. Morgan reached out and grabbed Alex's arm, digging her short fingernails into his skin.

Alex was frozen, staring at the man in the suit, even as he continued to lurch toward the diner, his leg almost broken in half. A bald trucker in a blue flannel shirt finally stepped outside and approached the man. He held out his hands saying, "Just sit down there, buddy. We'll get ya some help."

A waitress dialed 911 on her cell phone but cursed loudly when she got a busy signal. Just as the bald trucker reached out to touch the broken frame of the man in the suit, the body fell forward. Blood covered hands gripped onto the arms covered in blue flannel. The man in the suit pulled himself closer, his mouth open wide and his eyes showing only white orbs. The bald trucker tried to support him, but the man in the suit lifted himself, pulling his face up to the bald trucker's chest.

The bloody, wounded face lunged forward, mouth stretched open, baring broken, jagged teeth. Those teeth dug into the trucker's neck. He ripped and tore at the tough flesh until a hunk of bloody meat the size of a fist was pulled out in a stringy mess.

The customers in the diner all reeled back at the same time. Everyone screamed in fear and anger. The bloody man in the suit feasted on the hunk of meat and he let the trucker's body fall to the ground. When he finished chewing, he sniffed the air near the trucker and then turned toward the diner. He began his lurching movement, disregarding the body of the now-dead trucker all together.

Another trucker yelled, "That son of a bitch killed Chester!" This trucker had long curly red hair that matched his thick beard. He slammed the front door of the diner open, stomping out into the parking lot to confront the murderer.

A waitress yelled out, "No, Red! Don't!"

By the time she yelled, the red haired trucker was already outside and punching the man in the suit repeatedly in the face. The man fell to the ground, but kept struggling.

As Red continued to pound his fists into the now crushed skull of the man, the bald trucker with a bite out of his neck began to twitch in the snow.

"He's alive," Morgan gasped and pointed at the bald trucker's body. A waitress yelled at her phone from behind them. Still no answer from the emergency services.

The twitching trucker suddenly sat upright, blood still gushing from his wound. He scrambled to his feet and stepped toward Red, who was only now beginning to slow his assault. The murderer's skull was nothing more than a bloody, pulpy mess in the snow.

Red turned toward the twitching, bleeding man and jumped to his feet to help him. The bald trucker lunged forward, and Red tried to block the gaping mouth with his arm. The trucker's teeth sunk in to the meaty part of Red's forearm. The bald trucker ripped his teeth away, pulling strings of flesh and muscle with them. Red fell into the snow and the bald trucker in the blue flannel began chewing his mouthful, watching Red with the same white, lifeless eyes that the man in the suit had only seconds ago.

"Morgan, we need to get out of here," Alex said to her, never taking his eyes off the windows. The crowd was panicking, and Alex could feel the tension in the air.

"My car is out there." Her voice drifted off as she pointed out past the madness. The attacking trucker jumped on top of Red again, snapping his mouth open and closed like a crazed dog. Behind them was Morgan's Volkswagen. Two more truckers ran outside, trying to stop the mayhem. More blood was spilled, and Morgan's grip was beginning to turn Alex's arm numb.

Red, now showering the window in a spray of blood from his neck, slammed into the glass with his body. His mouth was open and his tongue swirled around on the glass. He moaned ,and gurgled through the blood in his throat. His hands pounded on the glass, smearing crimson hand prints on the icy exterior.

The men behind him, all of them covered in blood with gaping wounds that produced more red fluid every second, began moaning as well. Only the original man in the suit didn't move. His head was still in a liquid form from Red's fists.

The men who were moving ran toward the Diner, their mouths hanging open in a look of salivation. Two older men braced the doors, holding them closed so the crazed men outside couldn't get in. The two men yelled for someone to call the police. Red continued pounding his fists into the window. The glass began to splinter and more of the bloody men started to give up on the door and join his pounding.

"Holy shit," Morgan said bluntly. Alex backed away from the window and finally tore his eyes away from the carnage. He scanned the back of the diner and yanked Morgan toward the kitchen saying, "Come on, we need to get out of here."

Morgan did not argue.

The two of them pushed through swinging doors into the kitchen and they heard the cook yell at them to get out. They ignored the cook's demand and he gave up, focused more on the insanity happening in his parking lot.

The two made their way past the row of oven-tops and hanging fry-pans. They found a metal door in the very back. Taped to it was a red exit sign hanging crookedly. Alex pushed open the door and they both watched a pile of wet snow fall down from the roof. He immediately realized he had forgotten his coat. He began to turn back, but he heard the shatter of glass from the front of the diner and then the explosion of screams. Morgan turned and looked directly into his eyes, drilling her fear into his brain. He nodded, letting her know she need not explain, and they both ran out the back door, leaving the inhuman moaning sounds behind them.

The alley behind the diner was flanked by a wire fence that separated it from a small park. A dumpster was sitting right next to the back door and bags of trash lined the wall. Alex and Morgan both looked around cautiously, scanning through the blowing snow for any of the murderous men. Screams could be heard from inside the diner. Horrific screams.

Alex began to move to the right when a moan erupted from around the corner and a decrepit old man slowly staggered from the side of the building into the alleyway. He held his arms the same way as the others, reaching for the two of them with his mouth hanging open, but his body could only carry him so fast. Matching his age, he dressed in clothes from the early 1940's. Half his face was gone and only bone showed through. The old man staggered toward them.

Alex called out, "Hey! Hey, just leave us alone!"

Morgan added in, "We don't want any trouble."

The man continued approaching them. Behind him, out in the street, Alex saw a man get tackled by a woman. She tore into his chest with her teeth. Alex turned and looked into the panic stricken eyes of the girl he cared deeply for.

"Run," was all she said.

Alex saw a piece of fence that hung loose and he knelt down to it. Pushing it aside for Morgan, he said through gritted teeth, "Come on, through here."

Still holding onto each other's hands tightly, the two of them ran into the park and over the small hill that a tree sat at the top of. Their feet slipped on the snow covered grass periodically but their momentum kept them moving forward. When they reached the top they both spun around, surveying the streets that surrounded them. They could see random groups of people moving near the park and a few people running away from them. Screams and moans were carried on the howling wind. The sound of sirens could be heard faintly in the distance. The chaos was scattered, but grew with every passing second.

"What is happening, Alex?" Morgan panted, out of breath from running up the hill. "Why did those guys attack each other like that? This can't be just a flu virus."

"They were eating each other." Alex rubbed his eyes, no longer trusting them. "Why would they do that? What could make somebody do that?"

Morgan shook the snow from her hair and looked down. "I want my car. We need my car. We can't stay here."

"You're right." Alex looked around, smoke started to pour into the air from surrounding buildings that had caught on fire for unknown reasons. The chaos was spreading out in waves. His paranoia showed him the end of the world. Morgan screamed his name, shocking him out of his fantasies and alerting him to a small child running toward them. She was missing her arm and growling through bloody teeth.

"Oh my god, I'm going to puke." Morgan covered her mouth.

Alex looked down at the one armed girl as she tried to lift her feet high enough to walk through the deep snow. She kept coming toward them, wearing torn, stained, pink snow-pants. The sight of the blood covered child chilled him to his bones. His instinct was to help her. She was eight at the oldest.

Morgan had never seen a child so young with that look on her face. She ground her teeth together, making up her mind. The little girl posed no physical threat to her. A swift kick to the head and the kid would be tumbling down the hill. If the parents wanted to sue her, they could go right ahead.

"You're not going to eat us." Morgan stepped up and kicked as hard as she could, almost slipping on the ice but managing to fumble her arms in the air to keep her balance. Morgan's foot connected with the little girl's face and her tiny body went rolling down the hill, casting off the snow all around it. She never stopped hissing the entire way down the hill.

Morgan shrieked, "Oh my god. What did I-"

Without answering Alex grabbed onto Morgan's wrist and he pulled her toward the street. She resisted at first, but gave in easily, following his pull. When they reached the sidewalk, he ran in a straight and determined line back toward the parking lot.

"I kicked that little girl!"

"These people are insane and they're trying to kill people," Alex was speaking in a focused monotone explanation. In his mind, there was no room for error in his judgment. "You did the right thing. You were trying to help me."

"You're right." She breathed heavy and grabbed his shoulder, turning him so he was looking at her. "Thank you." He had reminded her of her strength. He had pulled her back into the space in her mind she was most comfortable. A cold place.

Alex turned back around, leading them toward the front of the diner. A small group of women began moaning in front of a store and they turned toward Alex and Morgan, lifting their arms outstretched in front of them. Alex started running again, pulling Morgan's arm behind him. Luckily, the three women became distracted by a family who was trying to unlock the doors of their minivan.

When Alex and Morgan finally reached the corner of the diner and peeked around at the parking lot, they saw it was beginning to fill with the infected. Morgan recognized most of the customers from inside the diner, now badly wounded, one even missing his leg. They all stumbled about, mindlessly staggering through the snow and broken glass.

Alex knew they couldn't get into the car without getting near at least some of the infected people, but he hoped Morgan could.

"I'm going to run through the parking lot and cause a distraction", Alex said, squinting his eyes to scan the entire lot. "When they come after me, run for your car. I'll circle around the back of the diner and you pick me up at the end of the alley."

"Alex, no..."

Without listening to her, he took off running. Her instinct was to yell at him, but she caught the words about to burst from her throat and she stayed hidden.

Alex ran into the lot, and before he even made a noise two waitresses began shrieking into the air. One of them was missing her bottom jaw and a tongue wriggled around in the exposed throat. She started moving toward him, climbing over knocked over chairs, still shrieking. The rest of the infected people turned to face him, alerted by the high pitched noise. He ran past the first two truck drivers easily, slamming his fists on the hoods of the cars to draw their attention.

Soon the whole lot was moaning, turning to run toward Alex. He leapt up onto the ice covered hood of a car, slipping, and almost falling off. Once he regained his balance he looked over the mass of people moving toward him. Some of them walked, some were running, and in the distance he saw Morgan spring from the corner of the diner and start for her car. The people stayed focused on him.

Smiling, he leapt off the hood and he ran for the side of the building, turning around to keep yelling at the infected people, drawing them closer.

He made his way to the back of the diner and he slid around the corner into the alleyway. Between him and the road stood the old man dressed in a suit from the 1940's. He moaned when he saw Alex and the old man started walking slowly toward him. Alex looked back and he saw the mass of diner customers still following his trail.

He looked down at the dumpster against the brick wall and he saw a plank of wood hanging loosely from a crate. He grabbed the wide board and pulled on it, trying to break it off. His first pull didn't even budge the board, but once he planted his foot into the side, the board pulled free. As he stepped back from the release, he saw the customers behind him round the corner, their moan reaching a sort of crescendo.

Alex turned from them, and he ran toward the old man, swinging the board behind his head like a baseball bat. Right before he reached a swinging distance in front of the flesh hungry old man, Alex's foot slipped out from underneath him and he found himself lying on his back with the wind knocked out of lungs.

As he stared into the sky, trying to suck air into his chest, the old man stepped over him, leaning down to grab him with long skinny fingers. Alex rolled to the side and he scrambled to his feet. He saw the customers running into the alley and he stepped back as the old man lunged for him.

He found himself with his back against the chain link fence and the old man was still coming. He dove under the old man's outstretched arms and he ran for the street. He felt the old man's fingers scrape against his back as he ducked by him and broke away free.

As he neared the opening of the alleyway, he saw Morgan's Volkswagen pull up. She leaned over and opened the door so that he could jump in. He did and he slammed the door behind himself. Alex hammered the lock with his fist and Morgan stomped on the gas as the mob of people slammed into her car, splattering their blood across the windows. The wheels spun in the ice before finally catching and launching them down the road. Alex realized then that he had been screaming the entire time. He was still screaming. His lungs tried to stop.

"Don't ever do something like that again," Morgan yelled and she started slapping his arm.

Morgan spun the car around on the ice, making a sharp right turn at high speed. She spun the car out straight again and she headed for the city limits, dodging around the random person running through the street.

She stopped herself from crying as they drove past a woman yelling for help. The woman was holding off one infected person, but two more were almost on top of her. No matter how many times Alex told her she did the right thing by continuing to drive, Morgan would never forgive herself.

AFTER LIFE

Day 1

12:32 pm

The radio offered nothing but speculation as they turned onto I-94, heading back to Alex's apartment. Morgan's house was closer, but she brushed off Alex when he asked why she didn't want to go there. The interstate was surprisingly empty and Morgan pushed past the speed limit without hesitation. She needed safety and she needed it now. Alex tried his cell phone over and over, but only got a recorded message about high call volume. His body was starting to feel weak as the adrenalin wore off. His arms felt tight and his tongue was dry.

"The President has issued a general health warning for all the 48 states." The hosts on the radio acted calm, which Alex felt guilty about wanting to believe. He wanted to think this was normal. He wanted to think if they just got home and locked the door, it would be no different than a bad blizzard.

He felt guilty that he could offer no solace, or comfort to Morgan. He wanted to badly. He knew they both needed it. *Is it really only fear that stops me? Fear that I would make her uncomfortable if I touched her,* he thought. *Or is it the fear that the temptation of simply touching her is too much for me?* Morgan bit her lip, her mind thinking of Christopher. She wondered if he was okay. She wondered if he was sick, or if these crazed people were at the airport. She wanted to voice her concern, but she held it in. She was unable to show Alex any vulnerability.

The radio filled the silence. "The number of dead is still an unknown factor at this time, but eyewitness accounts lead us to believe the number is very large, possibly reaching into the tens-of-thousands. Those suffering from fever, disorientation, suicidal or homicidal thoughts, or any type of psychotic behavior are urged to visit the hospital immediately. You can also visit our website and check our FAQ – that's frequently asked questions – about this new health phenomenon. And, now we have an expert in the field joining us. Dr. Julian Randolph, author of 'The Sickness of Madness.'"

"I'm scared Morgan." Alex had held that in since the first death.

Morgan had an unlit cigarette hanging in her mouth. She stared out the windshield, gripping the steering wheel tightly. Alex grabbed her lighter out of her hand on the steering wheel and he lit her cigarette for her.

"Thank you."

He tried to start a sentence, but spoke in fragments. "I'm... I don't mean... I just... This isn't just some sickness, you know? People weren't feeling pain. They were missing limbs, but the were still walking around."

"I know," she said dryly, taking another drag from her cigarette.

"They were attacking each other, but they didn't just want to hurt people."

"I know, Alex." She blew out her smoke hard, angrily.

"They wanted to bite you! To eat you!"

"I know, Alex!" That part she yelled. "I get it, okay? I was there. This is fucked up. This is totally... this is a total mess. I get it."

"I'm sorry." Alex shrunk into his seat. "You know me. I have to figure shit out. It always helped when I could do that. With you."

There was a silence in the car as those words hung in the air. Morgan let the sweetness of the comment sink into her chest. She took a deep breath.

"Alex." She took a drag of her cigarette. "Thanks for... thanks for everything back there." She reached out and grabbed his hand, squeezing it for only a moment.

Alex smiled, and he turned to look at Morgan, hoping to catch the look in her eye. She stared out the windshield, letting go of his hand. Alex turned slowly away from her and looked out his window. The sky over Minneapolis was beginning to fill with clouds of smoke. Small fires had broken out all over. Homes, businesses, cars, all of them sent plumes of billowing black pillars into the sky. The city looked like a war zone.

When they reached the exit, Morgan let out a whispered curse as they both noticed a grouping of people wandering down the middle of the ramp. The people turned as the car approached and started running as fast as they could, screaming in a bloody, gurgling growl. Morgan instinctively pressed on the brakes and the car began to slow.

"No!" Alex yelled, pressing the palms of his hands against the dashboard. "Don't slow down!"

Morgan screamed in disgust as a woman leapt onto the hood of the car, her eyes gouged from her face and her shirt torn open exposing her ripped apart chest. The woman's ribcage was opened wide, vital organs missing from the cavity.

Morgan pressed on the gas and the car sped forward, slamming into the side of a mailman with a red stained uniform. It continued on, knocking over a large man with no shirt, who's arm dangled at the elbow by a few layers of skin.

"What the fuck, Alex! Look at these people!" Morgan spun the wheel when they reached the top of the ramp, turning onto the two lane road at high speed. The bloody woman atop the hood slid off, her fingernails digging into the windshield and leaving behind a smear of red blood.

The road in front of them was scattered with people, many of them running at the car and beating their hands against the side as Morgan swerved in between them.

They reached the parking lot behind Alex's apartment, and both gasped a breath of relief when they saw no infected people. Morgan slammed on the brakes, hopping up onto the curb of the parking spot. They both jumped out of the car, and keys at the ready, Alex unlocked the back door to the building. Holding the door open for Morgan, he nearly fell into the doorway as he saw an infected man from the street come running around the corner, trying to spot what happened to the inhabitants of the Volkswagen. The stairwell door slammed shut, auto locking, just as the enraged man saw Alex in the doorway.

Alex started the climb up the three flights of stairs, leading the way. He bounded up the stairs, taking at least two stairs at a time. By the second floor Morgan called out: "Slow down" in between heaving breaths. Alex trotted back down a few stairs and put his hand on her back. He immediately yanked his hand away like he had touched a hot pan, instead just walking at a slower pace alongside her.

When they reached the third floor Alex pulled the door to the hallway open slowly and peeked through the opening as quietly as he could. The hallway looked empty so he pulled the door open fully and he waved his hand at Morgan, motioning for her to walk through.

She ducked under his arm that held the door and he followed her down the hallway once she passed through. They made their way to his apartment quietly and he fumbled with his keys once they got to the door. Finally he got the large key to slide into the lock and the door fell open. They both rushed in, gasping for breath they didn't realize they had been holding and Alex shut the door behind them. He locked the doorknob and the deadbolt.

Morgan took off her coat and she sat down on Alex's couch. She rested her head in her hands and she let her hair fall to the sides of her fingers. Alex walked into the kitchen and leaned against his counter top.

"We should turn on the news," he said quietly, not sure what he should say. A thought dawned on him and he began digging through the cupboards. Morgan pushed her hair behind her ears, adjusted her glasses, and reached out for the remote. As she clicked on the screen, Alex came back into the room with a small bowl. "You can use this as an ashtray."

"No. No. I'm not going to smoke in your apartment." She pushed the bowl away from her.

He laughed uncomfortably as he sat down in a recliner next to the couch. "Seriously. I'm not going to make you go outside."

Morgan chuckled and let out a sigh of defeat. She smiled when she thought of how nice he was being. She lit a cigarette.

"You should try to call you parents," Morgan said.

Alex cringed. Morgan's mother and father had died in a car crash fourteen months ago. His concern for his own parents felt selfish. He made a mental note to try to call later.

"Oh my god!" Morgan was staring at the TV while covering her mouth with her hand, but she didn't look away.

Alex looked at the screen and saw a home video of a man missing the lower half of his body crawling down a sidewalk. Intestines and hunks of flesh dragged behind him, but he left no blood trail. This man had lost all his blood a long time ago.

His flesh was mottled and saggy. He dragged himself at a slow pace, but continued pulling his upper half toward the cameraman. He had the same milky white look in his eye that all the infected did.

Across the bottom of the screen in blocky letters it read:

DEAD MAN STILL MOVES!

Morgan shook her head. "No way. There is no way. It's a hoax. It has to be."

Alex just kept watching the video, which they replayed over and over. "It looks real, Morgan. The people we saw on the street were almost as bad as he looks."

Morgan said nothing, still looking skeptically at the screen.

"Morgan. Holy shit. Morgan, it makes sense. Think about it. People biting other people? That guy who got hit by the truck and smacked his head? How did he get back up? Morgan."

"Don't even say it!"

"They're zombies."

Morgan rolled her eyes and threw her hands up in the air, "Of course you would think that."

Alex pointed at the TV screen. "How do you explain that? That dude is totally dead! That lady on your car didn't have any lungs!"

"Corpses twitching on the ground is not going to turn this virus into some voodoo horror film cliché. Give me a break, Alex. I don't want to joke around about this."

AFTER LIFE

"I'm not joking! That woman on your car was doing a lot more than twitching!"

Alex stared at Morgan with a very serious look on his face, trying to resist an urge. He finally gave in and walked over to the wall that his samurai swords hung on. He grabbed his favorite one and he carried it back over to the chair, keeping it next to him. Morgan burst out laughing.

"I'm not joking Morgan." Alex kept his chin pointed up, ignoring her continued laughter. "You can believe anything you want. What I see are god-damned zombies."

"Oh my god, Alex," Morgan just kept laughing. "I totally can't take you seriously right now." She stood up and walked to the window in his kitchen, looking out onto the street.

"Alex, come look at this."

Alex stood up, carrying his sword with him. He peeked over her shoulder and out the window. He saw three men walking across the street, looking in the window of an electronics store. One was missing an arm and the other two looked like police officers. All of them were covered in blood.

"Shit. Not even the cops are safe." Morgan checked her cell phone again with no luck and set it on the kitchen table. "So what do we do, just stay here until the TV tells us to come out?"

"If you want." Alex kept looking out the window. "You're totally welcome to stay. I don't want you going outside. Just seems like a bad idea until we figure this out."

"Well, I'm not going back to my empty house." Morgan dropped back onto the couch. "I guess we can just wait it out. Together."

Alex wanted to tell her that Christopher would be fine. He wanted to assure her that everything would go back to normal soon. Before he could speak, he watched the two infected officers and the one-armed man run across the street, chasing one of his neighbors and toward the front door of his apartment building.

"Yeah," he mumbled quietly, gripping the handle of his sword. "Together."

AFTER LIFE

Day 1

8:14 pm

Alex turned off the TV when the screams started downstairs. They sat in the living room as quietly as they could. Alex gripped the samurai sword tightly in one hand, and Morgan's hand in the other. Slowly, the screams had worked their way through the building. It did not take long for them to make it to the third floor. The sun was just setting, but Alex hadn't dared turn on any lights.

"I think I hear them next door," Morgan whispered. Alex could feel her shivering.

Alex held his breath, trying hard to listen to the silence, when something slammed into the wall separating his apartment from his neighbor's. The pictures on the wall rattled and then there was silence again.

Alex looked at Morgan and was about to say something when a moan came from the other side of the wall. An unmistakable moan that was low and quiet, yet so close. Alex knew that only the thin plaster separated them. An infected person stood only fifteen feet from where he sat.

"Alex." Morgan trembled, and he tried to pull her close. Her rigid body wouldn't budge. He moved closer to her, but still couldn't wrap his arm around her. He let the feeling of her body next to his thrill him, for only a moment.

Someone banged on the front door. It shook through the silence, nearly knocking them both out of their seat. Alex almost let out a yelp, but his breath was taken away and nothing came out. Instead, he slowly grabbed the handle of the sword, sliding it out of its sheath only a few inches.

A scream came from down the hall and they could both hear feet run away from Alex's apartment door in the direction of the screaming. They listened to the ghastly sounds of a old woman being torn apart two apartments away.

Minutes passed before the bang came again, startling them both. This time, the hands slid down the other side of the door, scraping slowly down to the floor.

Again and again, sometimes with minutes in between, the banging shook the door. For hours into the night the noise continued, randomly shocking them and making their bodies jump every time the sound broke the stillness.

Morgan spent hours simply staring at the door, using every muscle in her body to muffle the sound of her breathing. Alex sat in the darkness with the sword in his hand, staring at the door, waiting for it to open. He soon needed to set the sword on the floor because his body began to shake so uncontrollably that the metal on the handle of the sword began to rattle.

By the time morning came, the two of them had lost track of when the last bang had been heard. Alex thought it was only a few minutes ago, but Morgan insisted it was at least an hour. This argument they wrote on a piece of paper, still horrified to make any noise at all. They spent the morning and afternoon like this, writing in a notebook back and forth.

Morgan's nerves made her become more hostile as midday approached, but she still could not bring herself to smoke. She could only assume the infected people could still smell. Her notes to Alex became more agitated. Even her letters were written more sharply.

> *Do you want me to check the hallway?*
> *No!*
> *I'm going to. Maybe they left.*
> *No! Absolutely not!*
> *We can't be quiet forever. I have to know.*
> *Put your sword away! You are not a ninja!*
> *We have to do something.*
> *You are not going to kill anybody!*
> *What if they come in here?.*
> *Let's put something in front of the door. Your bookshelf!*

Alex let out a sigh and he put the sword down. He looked over at his bookshelf and smiled. He had built it himself, and it reached from the floor to the ceiling, almost covering one entire side of his apartment.

The bookshelf was a second wall. If they wanted to keep something out, Morgan was right, that would keep them out.

Alex threw his hands into the air and stood up, walking over to the bookshelf. Morgan smiled a winning smile and stood up to help him push. After thirty minutes of pushing the shelf inch by inch, they finally tipped over the solid wood frame so that it slammed into and rested firmly against the front door. Moans came from the hallway outside when the first noises of movement happened, but when the shelf fell into place, they both felt instantly safer.

"That should keep them out," Alex finally said, almost scaring himself with his own voice.

"You think it's safe to talk?" Morgan still whispered.

"We could barely slide that thing, there is no way they're lifting it off the door." Alex patted the giant bookshelf, proud of his construction. A moan came from the other side of the door. Alex pulled his hand off as if the shelf was what made the noise. "Let's move the desk over here just in case."

When they finished moving the desk, they both collapsed on the couch. They sat on opposite ends, but turned toward each other, their feet almost touching.

"I'm so tired," Alex said. When he looked at Morgan, her eyes were already closed. He got up and found her a blanket. He placed the afghan over her gently, slowly pulled her glasses off her face and set them on the coffee table.

He turned on the TV, pushing on the volume button to keep it as quiet as possible. His body told him to sleep, his back aching from staying in one position all night.

But, his mind needed to know.

He needed to know what was happening.

AFTER LIFE

Day 2

1:41 pm

The news anchor looked as though he hadn't slept either. Bags under his eyes were barely covered by smeared makeup. His hair looked tussled, as if his fingers had been pulling at it all night. He read aloud from a pile of papers in front of him instead of a teleprompter. Other station workers ran past in the background, holding stacks of papers in their hands, rushing breaking news to the control room. The room that the anchor broadcast from was in a state of chaos.

"General Bellstone offered no comment on the military's placement within the United States, or a possible withdrawal from the Middle East. Republican Senator Bill Levitch has issued a statement asking for an emergency meeting of Congress to correlate a strategy with Homeland Security and the Military. He has hopes that both will work together to create a quarantine for America's borders." The anchor set down the newspaper, shaking his head. "I fear, from what we have gathered across the nation, that it may be too late to shut down our borders. I want to restate our list of known facts for viewers that... that may just be tuning in."

The news anchor took a sip of water and he ran his fingers through his hair as he grabbed a piece of orange paper that was set to the side.

"FEMA centers are still being set up outside major metropolitan areas." The anchor looked off camera. "Can we run that list on the bottom of the screen, Phil? Yes? Okay. We urge people to use caution when traveling to the centers. FEMA has issued a statement saying they are doing their best to screen everyone coming in for infection, but we have already gotten word from Phoenix, Arizona of an outbreak within the center walls. Police there are doing everything they can but citizens near the center have been asked to stay within their homes until the center can be cleared of any threats."

Alex watched the bottom of the screen and saw Hudson, Wisconsin roll past. It wasn't far from Minneapolis, but the idea of leaving his apartment sent a chill down his back. He looked to the peacefully sleeping Morgan next to him and he knew he was exactly where he wanted to be.

"We can now confirm that many European cities have also seen an infection, as well as China, Japan, India, Australia, and many cities in South America. The infection is global and appears to be targeting people at random. There has been no connection between those infected and anything they have come in contact with."

The news anchor began reading the next line when a man ran in from the left side of the screen and whispered into his ear as he handed him a piece of paper. The anchor looked at the man and mouthed the words, "Are you sure?" The man nodded, glanced into the camera, and quickly ducked back to the left.

"Um, folks, it looks like we have some new information coming in from the Center for Disease Control." The anchor reread the paper in front of him and began

AFTER LIFE

running his fingers through his hair again. "The CDC has issued the following statement to the Associated Press, and we just received it over the wire only moments ago. I... I'm having a hard time with this..."

A voice could be heard yelling at the anchor off-camera, but was muffled because of the distance from the microphone. "This can't be true Phil! It must be a hoax!" The voice yelled back and the anchor let out a deep sigh, holding up his hand in defeat.

"The CDC, after testing hundreds of patients, has concluded that symptoms are only showing up in patients that have already... in patients that are dead. Once the heart has stopped in a patient, they have witnessed a reactivation of brain activity in less than one minute and no more than ten minutes. The brain activity is limited and results in sporadic muscle control, homicidal aggression, and possibly even... cannibalism."

The anchor took another sip of water. "I'm sorry folks, I just..." He rubbed his fingers on the bridge of his nose, between his eyes and continued. "They cannot explain the rapidness of the outbreak, but have speculated that international flights and rapid transit could have spread the infection before anyone was aware of it. They also claim to have no reports of anything like this happening in the past and are shocked at the sudden uprising of cases. The CDC has not been able to recognize what is causing the brain reactivation, but has not ruled out anything. They urge those who come in contact with the infected to stay away from any blood or saliva and to clean any open wounds thoroughly."

The anchor picked up the orange sheet again and attached the CDC report to it with a paper clip.

"Continuing our list of facts: I want to re-state that this is information we know for sure. Speculation at this point is dangerous. Extremely dangerous. The White House issued a statement notifying us that the President is in perfect health and has been moved to an undisclosed location. The

Vice-president, who was visiting foreign leaders in Mumbai when the outbreak happened, is on his way to the airport and hopes to be back in the United States by tonight. Any and all enlisted soldiers are required to check-in with their superior officers for information. The President has issued an executive order activating all troops, even non-active duty reservists. Military ground personnel have been officially reported in New York, but all other eyewitness accounts are still being confirmed. Cell phone and LAN based telephone services across the globe have been shut down for military and government use, but most Internet connections are still available. White House officials are urging people to take advantage of e-mail and social networking sites to contact loved ones."

The man flipped the sheet of the paper over and started reading from the back. "Within the last three hours, the White House issued a statement in reply to many user comments on the Internet about self-defense from the infected. The government is standing by the previous ruling of brain-death as being the determination of death, and has stated that all infected individuals are still considered living beings and therefore deserving of every law and right belonging to them. Anyone committing an act of violence toward these citizens will be held accountable. Any criminal acts perpetrated by the infected will be resolved in a court of law."

Alex hit the power button on the remote. His eyelids felt like they weighed a few pounds each and the news was telling him nothing he didn't already know. The government was fumbling to react to the crisis and he didn't trust them anymore now than he had in the past.

Possibly less.

He grabbed his laptop, scanning the few blogs he subscribed to for any information but found nothing new that wasn't a rumor. He sent out a mass email to all of his contacts letting them know that he and Morgan were okay and what their situation was. He asked anyone still healthy enough to reply, to do so as soon as they could.

He set the laptop down on the coffee table and walked into his bedroom. The afternoon light was beginning to fade. His bed looked soft and comfortable, but he couldn't resist one last look out the window. The streets were fuller than before, people wandering aimlessly, randomly searching for victims. He wondered what stopped them from attacking each other as he fell onto his bed.

He lay there, staring at the ceiling, suddenly unable to sleep. His mind washed back and forth between the infection that had him locking himself in his apartment, and the fact that Morgan was sleeping in the next room.

Alex smiled, allowing himself to fantasize about her for only a moment. He imagined what a date would be like with her. He imagined their conversations late at night, after they had made love. He imagined making love. All these fantasies existed in a world without Christopher and he was suddenly sickened by his fantasies.

Besides, he thought, *All that stuff can only exist in a world that still made sense. A world in which it was still safe to walk outside.*

As soon as he fell asleep, his body jerked awake when he heard someone say his name. His vision focused in and he saw Morgan holding her blanket around her shoulders, staring at him from his bedroom doorway.

"Alex?" she said again. "I'm sorry to wake you up."

"It's okay. What's wrong?" He rubbed his eyes, trying to make himself more aware.

"I'm just. I'm scared sleeping out there. Can I sleep in here?"

He tried to hold back his smile. "Yeah, absolutely." He started to pull back the covers to let her crawl in next to him, but she laid on the floor and pulled her blanket up around her. He mentally scolded himself for his assumption and handed her a pillow.

"Goodnight, Morgan." He lay on his side, watching her body raise and fall slowly in the little light that crept through his plastic blinds. Her breathing lulled him to sleep.

Neither of them slept soundly. While they both slept deeply, exhausted from their night before, they couldn't help waking up periodically with the myriad of noises that erupted around them. Screams, sirens, gunshots, and explosions filled their slumber.

AFTER LIFE

Day 2

6:30 am

While Morgan and Alex tried to sleep, a whole world was fighting for its survival outside. Morgan eventually felt guilty about this and woke up, quietly creeping into the living room to smoke. The smell of her cigarette woke Alex up and he came stumbling out of his room, rubbing his eyes.

"How did you sleep?" he asked, yawning the word *sleep*.

"Like shit," she said, releasing a lungful of smoke. "You?"

"I managed to sleep for a while, I guess that's what's important." He stumbled over to the living room and dropped his body into the recliner.

"I grabbed one of your shirts. I hope you don't mind. My shirt was-"

"No, it's cool. Take whatever you need."

"I just about screamed this morning when I realized you didn't have any coffee." Morgan laughed, only half joking.

"Oh wow, I didn't even think of that." He spoke in a rough voice and got up to get something to drink. "How many cigarettes do you have left?"

"Don't even ask…"

Alex came back into the room holding a can of soda. "You want caffeine?"

"Oh god, yes." Morgan gripped the can with both hands like she was receiving communion.

Alex sat back down with his own soda and grabbed the remote for the TV. He punched the power button with his thumb and made the screen spark to life.

The words "Zombie Attack!" were sprayed across the top of the screen while a montage of Internet movies played on loop. The videos were from all over the world, capturing eyewitness accounts of very dead people doing very living things.

"Again, these corpses seem to be reacting through what some experts have dubbed 'muscle memory.'" The voice-over sounded dull and bored. Obviously she had repeated this same script many times throughout the night. "The bodies are continuing to receive input from the brains, even though by all medical explanation, the brain should be dead."

Alex looked at Morgan, raising his eyebrows high into the air, pointing at the screen, and asking in a high-pitched voice, "What did I say?"

"They're just talking about theories. Who are these so-called experts. They aren't telling us anything." Morgan blew off what Alex thought was obvious fact. "Don't fall for this, Alex."

"Last night they said the CDC was saying that-" Alex shook his head, feeling it was too early to argue. "Forget it, do you want some breakfast?"

AFTER LIFE

"God yes, I'm starving."

Alex started rummaging through his cupboard and opened his fridge, pulling out a carton of eggs. He started scrambling them with some pulled apart slices of cheese. He could hear moans through the wall. It sounded like there were more infected people in the hallway.

"Can we turn on some music?" Morgan asked. "I need to try and drown out these noises."

"Yeah," Alex yelled from the kitchen. "My laptop controls the stereo."

Morgan opened his laptop and double clicked on the music icon. She sorted through his music folder and double clicked on the Trip-Hop genre. Smooth bass lines and scratching turntables mixed through the apartment, calming the entire room.

She double clicked on the Internet icon and opened the web browser. Alex's homepage greeted her with the top news stories of the day.

Looting rampant in major cities

World-wide mass homicides linked to drugs, disease, and the devil. Official word: We don't know the cause.

Survivors say: Hospitals are the worst place to be.

President to America: Stay in your home

Nationwide curfew now in effect.

Alex looked outside and saw nearly forty infected people wandering in front of the building. More walked around the surrounding streets. Fires continued to rage in the distance and he wondered how quickly they would spread to his building. His mind wanted desperately to feel safe, but his paranoia was strong.

Morgan heard a pounding on the wall. The pounding kept coming, changing patterns. She even heard the yelling of a man next door. She turned up the music and kept looking though the news stories.

"It says," Morgan yelled over the music into the kitchen, "that every report coming in describes the attacks as bites."

"If they aren't zombies, why are they trying to eat people?" Alex yelled back. "Cannibalism? What virus causes that?"

"It's not just that. The reports say that as soon as the person dies, the people don't try to bite them anymore." Morgan was sickened at the thought. "It's like they only want fresh meat."

Alex stepped into the room. "It makes sense Morgan. That's why it's spreading so fast. Those are all corpses. As soon as they kill, they move on. Another member of their army."

"Corpses." Morgan stared at the news article, scrolling through the story, but not really reading anything on the screen. "I mean, I guess, theoretically it's possible." She shook her head, unable to accept the idea.

Morgan clicked on Alex's blog subscriptions and started scanning the headlines. Rolling her eyes when she saw he had updates from a nude celebrity site and scrolling past the collection of video game blogs, she finally found something more newsworthy.

With a click, a British news site opened in front of her, displaying chilling words at the top of the screen.

NATO To Troops: Shoot To kill

British Prime Minister: We are exploring Nuclear options.

London Quarantine Fails

AFTER LIFE

Alex turned suddenly as he walked into the living room from the kitchen, glancing into his bedroom. His eyes grew large and he screamed, "What the hell?"

He immediately grabbed for the samurai sword that leaned against the wall. Morgan jumped up, following his gaze to the window in his room and screamed when she saw a man crawling in from the fire escape.

The man was overweight and had caught his jacket crawling in the window. Alex unsheathed the sword and held it out in front of him, readying himself to stab the man.

"No, don't," a voice yelled from out on the fire escape. Morgan looked through the window and saw a teenage girl looking past the man.

From his awkward position the man grunted out the words, "Alex! It's me! Mike. Mike Peterson!"

"Mr. Peterson?" Alex looked shocked, but relaxed the point of his sword. "What the hell are you doing?"

"We heard your music. We tried to pound on the wall to get your attention, but you couldn't hear us over the music." He struggled to get his jacket free. "So we crawled over from our fire escape. Luckily your window was open."

"Yeah." Alex frowned. "*Luckily*."

"Come on, man. Help me out, I look like an asshole."

Alex set the sword down on the floor and walked over to the window. He lifted the jacket off the hook on the window and Mr. Peterson tumbled onto the floor. Alex helped his daughter, Emma, through the window while her father pulled himself to his feet.

"Holy shit, right?" Mr. Peterson's face was red with exhaustion and embarrassment as he straightened out his jacket and shirt. "I mean… people are freakin' eating each other out there. This is some crazy shit, am I right?" He slapped Alex in the chest with the back of his hand.

Alex looked down at where he had been slapped and walked over to pick up his sword. He turned around, now standing right next to Morgan. In his most droll voice Alex replied, "Yes Mr. Peterson, this is some crazy shit."

"We-he-hell, Alex my boy, I ain't never seen this pretty lady come round before." The overweight man stepped closer to Morgan, looking her up and down while he licked his lips under his mustache and wiped his sweaty forehead. "Not bad, little man. Not bad at all."

"Did you need something, Mr. Peterson?" Alex was completely grossed out by the man and wanted him out of his house as fast as possible.

"Well, we really just wanted to make sure you were alive, Alex. See if ya needed anything."

Before Alex could say no, Morgan asked, "Do you have coffee?"

Mr. Peterson smiled a big grin, "Now that depends on what you have for *me*."

Alex stepped forward. "So you're not here to help, you just want something."

Mr. Peterson frowned, feigning his shock. "Alex! No, no. We're neighbors right? I'm just glad to see you're alive! We need to help each other out."

"We have eggs. And the Internet." Morgan was mentally betting Mr. Peterson used dial-up, which was useless when the phone lines were tied up.

"The eggs sound good. But what the hell would I need the Internets for? You got any beer?"

Morgan had underestimated how much of a luddite Alex's neighbor actually was.

"No," Alex answered. "We don't have any beer."

Mr. Peterson scratched his chin, thinking. "Give me a dozen eggs and I'll give you two pots of coffee."

"I only have six left," Alex said.

Mr. Peterson smiled at Morgan. "Unless you have something else to offer, that'll only get you one pot."

"If you just crawled over here to try to sell us things, you can head back home, Peterson." Alex lifted his sword.

AFTER LIFE

Mr. Peterson looked down at the sword and chuckled. "Nice sword, Alex. Looks like some piece of Jap shit."

He turned and walked back toward the window, his daughter started to climb out and she silently mouthed the words "I'm sorry" to them.

"If you change your mind, we're right next door. Shit is rough out there, Alex. We need to stick together. Help each other out. You need to provide for your woman, and I have plenty of food to provide her with." He winked at Morgan.

"Thanks for the offer, Mr. Peterson," Alex mumbled as he slammed the window closed behind the large man and dropped the blinds shut. He turned to Morgan and motioned toward the dresser. "Can you help me push that in front of the window until I can find some wood to nail over it?"

"Absolutely." Morgan shivered, a look of disgust on her face.

Day 8

5:22 pm

On the fifth day of the infection, the news stopped. All that was shown for the next three days on every station was the logo of the Emergency Broadcast System. It listed the official web pages to go to for more information at the bottom of the screen. With the news channels not receiving any updates they had resorted to repeating facts, speculating with anyone in the studio that had some wild idea, and replaying the same videos, showing the same people being attacked over and over.
Alex did not find himself missing it.
Morgan scrolled through Alex's DVD collection on his hard drive for what felt like the millionth time. Still, she found herself excited to watch the next movie with him.
After deconstructing every masterpiece of film-making with Christopher, it felt nice to watch something mindlessly action packed with Alex and laugh at the horrible

acting. She found herself anything but bored and she hadn't left the couch in three days.

They had never spent this much time together. Never given endless amounts of free time to talk about any silly subject that popped into their head. The conversations tended to center around the devastation they could witness from the window and heated debates about what was "really going on".

The discussion about whether to stay put or try to make it to a FEMA camp lasted all of six seconds. Morgan could only assume Christopher's plane had taken off already and that he wouldn't still be in the area. Alex had watched the groupings of infected grow from the few wandering around on the street to the mob of them that covered every inch of open space outside the building and she now realized they didn't have a chance outside. Between the infected and the source of the gunfire that popped in the distance, the outside world had become a death trap.

The infected filled the streets and alleyways, bumping into each other as they moved in aimless directions, a seething mass of flesh eating corpses, moaning in hunger. The hallway outside the apartment was filled with them too. Alex and Morgan watched movies loud and cranked the music. Alex had even downloaded ambient noises to play while they slept.

Anything to keep the sound of the walking dead out of their dreams.

Without the news on TV, the Internet became a constant source of information and speculation. Even the major news sites were updated so frequently that information changed as soon as you read it. They nearly wore out the F5 key refreshing the pages.

One site claimed the FEMA camps had fallen and that even the President was dead. They talked of underground movements that had formed in Montana and Canada, but were hopeless in their headlines for America.

Another reported the exact opposite. According to them, the Military had things under control and were only now regaining major cities in an effort to reestablish order. They spoke to many officials who claimed the president was feeling very healthy and would unveil his strategic plan soon.

Reports of the military's presence were updated constantly, with Internet posters tracking any movement near them. Alex and Morgan could hear the rattle of machine-gun fire and the occasional concussion of an explosion miles away. Jets flew over constantly, but the fighting was always in the distance.

Both Alex and Morgan had sent out emails to everyone they knew, but had yet to get a reply. Morgan checked more often than Alex, sure that Christopher had brought his laptop with him.

Even without a response, she refused to give up hope.

On one random instance, Alex had somehow received a phone call. It was an automated message from Wal-Mart, letting him know he was late for his shift. Morgan had to restrain him from throwing the phone out the window.

They spent time talking about their friends, which ones would have been at work, and which ones were at home. They both found themselves unable to comprehend how many people from their lives were most likely gone. They comforted each other with meaningless words of reassurance. It did not take them long to realize they were denying the truth. Their minds were simply unable to cope with the reality outside.

After talking about death for so long they both reached for simpler subjects they could discuss and maybe even laugh at.

They reached for any distraction.

That particular morning, the weather had changed to a more seasonable temperature. It actually started to look like May outside. The green trees and lush grass were a

AFTER LIFE

sharp contrast to the death and destruction around them. It was like nature was ignoring the apocalypse.

With the warmer weather, Alex needed to open the windows. As he started lifting the glass, the sounds of the city flooded into the apartment. He physically cringed at the low murmur of moans and the erratic sounds of violence that filled the air. The noise was only broken occasionally by a painful scream. But the screams came less often now. Anyone who had survived this long, was most likely somewhere safe. Somewhere that could withstand this onslaught.

"I want to watch this," Morgan said, and clicked on a movie icon. The logo for "Venezuela Vacation" came onto the screen, accompanied by the theme music.

"Yeah okay, it's a funny movie," Alex said, sitting down on the couch next to her.

"This sucks." Morgan sighed. "You've seen all these movies."

Alex suddenly felt incredibly sad as a thought dawned on him. He realized at that moment that there may no longer be new movies. His favorite actors may have been infected and killed. His favorite directors, too. Film was now a finite resource.

"Do you think Britney Spears is infected?" Morgan asked, lighting one of the cigarette butts in the ashtray, obviously having a similar thought as Alex.

Alex guiltily laughed. "What? I don't know. She lives in like, a gated house. With security. She probably had a good chance."

"When this is over we should start a website with, like, an updated list of the celebrities that were infected."

Alex shook his head. "That is seriously gruesome."

Morgan acted dramatically apologetic and appalled at her own behavior, waving her hands in the air. "Oh my god, I'm sooo sorry! The world is infected with reanimated corpses who devour the flesh of the living, and my joke about dead celebrities went too far, huh?"

Alex was laughing so hard he had to hold his stomach.

"I'm sorry Alex, did my attempt to lighten the mood offend your delicate sensibilities?"

"Okay, okay. I get it." Alex laughed, holding his hand up in surrender.

A sound dinged from his laptop, letting Alex know he had new mail. His laughter cut short, his eyes locked with Morgan's and they both jumped forward to look at the laptop. His hand clicked the mail icon and it displayed the new message.

To: Warriorpoet@hackmail.com
From: Venisonman@worldmail.com
Subject: Re: Anyone still alive?

Alex! My neighbor let me use his computer. He has satellite. I can't get my dial-up to work. Can you fix it? I was glad to hear from you. I'm still alive. Not a lot of people out here and I have a lot of guns. The people still breathing are more trouble than the ones who are dead. Ha ha. If you can make it here it is safer than the city. Keep in touch.
Dad.

Alex re-read the message, hoping he had read it right. He checked the time stamp to make sure it had been sent today. His eyes began to well up with tears.

Morgan leaned over and hugged him. "I'm so happy for you."

"My dad. I should have known he would survive." Alex laughed through his tears. His father was an outdoorsman, living in a small town in Wisconsin. The old man had three cabinets full of guns and Alex knew his house would be well protected. His father would have no problem killing to defend his home. He felt a twinge of embarrassment when he remembered arguing with his father over gun laws.

Alex looked over at his sword. He knew when the time came that he would hesitate. It had nothing to do with the laws the government had laid down. In his mind there was no denying that these people were already dead.

But they are still people, he though. *Or at least look like them.*

They are just bodies, he told himself.

Corpses.

Morgan set her hand on Alex's shoulder, seeing his eyes wander off into his own thoughts. She leaned in and asked, "Do you want to go to him?"

Alex was shook out of his trance and looked at Morgan. "In Wisconsin? Like, travel to Wisconsin? No." He almost laughed at the idea. "Absolutely not."

"Are you sure? I mean, he's your Dad."

"I'm sure," Alex said. "My dad would rather me be alive than be in Wisconsin." It made him feel safer, knowing someone he knew had survived. He was able to fall back into the defensive idea that all the horrible things he saw happening on the news were happening to other people. He paused, smirking. "Besides, I'm having too much fun with you."

As soon as the last word fell from his lips, the power blinked out in the apartment. The lights turned dark, the TV screen changed to black, and the music silenced.

"Alex?" Morgan said randomly, unsure of what she was asking.

"Oh man," Alex said, looking out the window, down the street. In the morning sun it was hard to tell if any lights were still on. "I guess I'm surprised it lasted this long…"

"Hey!" A voice yelled through the wall, "Hey, Alex! Did your power just go out?"

Alex recognized Mr. Peterson's muffled yell and yelled back, "Yeah."

"Fuck," was all he heard from the other side.

"Without power do we still have water?" Morgan asked, walking into the kitchen.

"Oh no," Alex said, the weight of her question suddenly dawning on him.

Morgan turned the faucet on and nothing happened. Her heart sank, immediately taking stock in her mind of how much soda Alex had in his refrigerator.

"Alex-"

"I know." He cut her off. "This is bad."

"What are we going to do?" she asked, not really expecting him to know.

"We need to at least look in the other apartments before it gets dark. See if we can search any of them or-" Alex paused, trying to let his brain focus. "But it's going to be dangerous."

Somehow, thinking of his father defending his childhood home inspired something inside of him. A sense of masculinity. Of power. If his father could do it, so could he. They would survive.

"We have no choice though." Morgan asked, "Right?"

Alex shrugged.

Morgan put her arm around him, squeezing him closer. "Have I told you how glad I am I get to go through this with you?"

Alex chuckled uncomfortably. "I wouldn't want to see the end of the world with anyone else."

"I'm serious!" Morgan said.

"So am I."

She sat back down calmly, smiling up at him. His mouth quivered into a crooked smile while he became lost in her eyes. There was an uncomfortable silence.

For Alex the silence lingered for too long.

AFTER LIFE

He walked over to the bedroom doorway saying, "I think I'm going to open up the fire escape window." He was obviously changing the subject. "We can see what's in the apartments that we can reach from there."

Morgan was both angry and thankful for his distraction. "Yeah, that sounds good. We can just search them one at a time. Take it slow."

Alex picked up his sword and started to buckle it on his belt.

He dug in his closet and found an old backpack from the semester he spent in college. A wasted 4 months spent in computer classes, trying to learn how to code so he could design his own video-games. He did well in the classes and the coding came easy to him, but the process bored him. He was also forced to see Morgan and Christopher every day, so dropping out was an easy choice.

A job at Wal-Mart greeted him when he left.

He emptied the bag and tossed it to Morgan, saying, "You can use that one." Alex stood up and grabbed his laptop bag, pulling all the wires and adapters out of the pockets. He slung it over his shoulder and shrugged at Morgan.

"Do you want a sword?" Alex asked sincerely, motioning toward his wall of cheaply made replicas of medieval weaponry.

"I don't think so." Morgan said, and picked up a metal candle holder he had displayed on his TV. The holder was long and had a heavy base. Held upside down it made a solid metal club. "This will work fine," she said, swinging the candle holder in the air.

They both moved the dresser that was set against the window and climbed out onto the fire escape. Morgan looked down at the alleyway below them and saw twenty of the infected people wandering through the back street. She couldn't believe the number of them and how much it had grown in only a few days. She couldn't imagine there were many people left in the city to infect.

As she scanned the group near the back wall, she saw a charred and blackened corpse lying next to a metal box attached to the building. The body's head was blown open on the top, its eyeballs nothing more than exploded goo. Power lines came down from a pole in the alleyway and attached to the box. The box looked charred as well.

Morgan pointed at the box and the body saying, "Looks like we know why the power went out."

Alex wondered how long it would take for the whole city to lose power.

They both climbed down the metal ladder to the next landing on the fire escape. Alex held his face up to the window and cupped his hands around his eyes, trying to peer through the glass into the apartment. All he could see was a bedroom with an unmade bed and dirty clothes lying on the floor.

He tried to lift the window, but it was locked tight. Morgan gently pushed him to the side and shattered the window with one good swing of her metal candle holder. She smiled when she saw the shocked look on Alex's face.

The men on the ground started to moan and reach up into the air when they heard the window shatter and saw the fresh meat above them.

Alex reached through the broken window and unlocked it, allowing him to lift the frame. The loose glass fell away when he moved it. Climbing through first, he unsheathed his sword and crept toward the living room.

Morgan stepped through the window behind him. She could tell a single man lived in the house by the bedroom. A laundry basket filled with nothing more than T-shirts and boxer shorts lay next to the bed. A magazine with a random female celebrity in a bikini was set next to the bedside lamp. A part of her felt like a detective. The other part felt like a criminal.

AFTER LIFE

Alex poked his head into the living room, glancing around the room. He motioned for Morgan to move up and she crept in close behind him.

"It looks clear," he whispered, but they both immediately heard a moan come from the kitchen when he spoke.

Alex peeked out the doorway again, only to see a woman lurch out of the kitchen, dried blood all over her chin and chest. Her head lashed around as she searched for the source of the noise, but she quickly saw Alex standing in the bedroom doorway.

Her eyebrows arched into points and her mouth dropped open, releasing a horrific scream. She lunged at him, her arms outstretched. He brought up his sword, reflexively defending himself. The point of the sword plunged into the woman's stomach, piercing through her back. She fell to the base of the sword and latched onto Alex's shoulders. Her mouth fell to his neck, only to get knocked away by Morgan's swinging candle holder.

Morgan brought the metal base down again onto the woman's arms, snapping one of her forearms in half. Jagged bone fell to the floor and Alex was released from her grip. As he pulled away, he gave a tug on his sword, breaking the handle off of the blade.

The woman lunged with the remaining good arm, grabbing onto Morgan's shirt. Morgan brought the candle holder up, smashing the wide base into the woman's jaw, snapping the mouth shut as the head reeled back from the impact.

Alex reached out and grabbed the woman's hair, yanking her head away from Morgan. The woman snapped her teeth and growled like a wild animal. Morgan kicked her feet out, pushing herself away from the woman. Once she was out of the woman's reach, the woman spun around and grabbed onto Alex, tackling him to the floor.

Alex slammed one hand under her jaw, holding her face away from his. The woman's drool started running down his hand as she foamed at the mouth, uncontrollably grabbing at his body.

He pushed as hard as he could and lifted her head up into the air. With a low crack, Morgan's candle holder smashed into her head, sending the body flying across the room. The woman stood back up immediately, her head dented in on one side.

"I'll hold her down!" Alex yelled, leaping at the woman. "You keep smashing!"

He jumped at her, bringing her to the floor and put all his weight on her shoulders. The woman kept lifting her head, only using her neck, trying to get herself within biting distance.

"Do it, Morgan! Do it now!"

"Oh my god!" Morgan turned her head away from what she knew she needed to do.

"Do it!"

Morgan brought the metal base down in a wide arc, crushing the woman's skull under her swing. Her face shattered into the floor, spraying the gore of her brains all over Alex and the carpet. When she lifted the candle holder off the impact site, strings of goo dripped from its bottom.

"I'm going to be sick," Morgan said, her face turning pale.

Alex looked down at the now headless woman, his sword blade still sticking out from her stomach. Her face was in pieces, splattered into the carpet in globs of fractured shards of bone. Alex could still recognize the body as his neighbor's girlfriend.

He looked down at himself and saw the woman's blood and brains all over his shirt. He could feel the hunks of flesh hanging in his hair. His mind wrestled with his body. One wanted to assess the situation and be happy he survived the encounter. The other wanted to release his lunch, adding to the disgusting mess in front of him.

He eventually gained control of his arms and pushed himself away, stumbling into the living room. Morgan was closing the door to the apartment, locking the deadbolt. The wood of the door was splintered around the doorknob, showing Morgan exactly how the infected had gotten into the apartment. Moans came from down the hall as nearby zombies began to respond to the commotion in the apartment. The doorknob hadn't been enough, but the deadbolt would keep them out. At least for a while.

Alex pulled off his shirt and used the back of it to wipe the gore from his head. *None in my eyes. None in my mouth. I'll be fine. I'll be fine.* He considered searching the man's room for a new shirt, but saw the body still lying on the floor and decided it was warm enough to remain shirtless for a little longer.

"Let's just get some food and whatever else we can find, and get out of here."

Alex watched Morgan try to move her shaking hands to open drawers and cupboards. He wanted to help her, but she looked like if he touched her she might shatter. She fumbled with canned vegetables and ravioli, filling her bag with the boxed food diet of the single male. Her arms felt weak, her head felt dizzy.

Alex stepped behind her and placed his hand on her shoulders. "Are you okay?"

"I'm just... that was..."

"I know."

"It felt just like killing."

"I know." His voice trailed off. He knew that woman was dead before they ever came into her apartment, but the experience had felt so real. It felt like murder, and he knew he would never be the same.

Morgan slung the backpack over her shoulder saying, "Forget it. I'm fine. I just need to get out of here," and walked back into the bedroom, exiting out the window.

Alex sat alone in the room, listening to Morgan's footsteps on the fire escape as she climbed back upstairs, and the moans of the corpses who stood right outside the door. He continued rooting through the drawers of the kitchen and finally dragged a chair over to the refrigerator to check the cupboard above it.

As he opened the doors of the small cupboard, a smile drew across his face. There, displayed in front of his curious eyes, were seven different bottles of alcohol. Various flavored vodkas, whiskey, and rum.

He did not realize it until that point, but it was exactly what he had been looking for.

AFTER LIFE

Day 11

8:20 pm

Alex sipped from the bottle of whiskey, rubbing his eyes as the liquid burned down his throat. He felt a bit selfish, drinking by himself on the rooftop, but he knew Morgan hated whiskey. His eyelids were growing heavy, but the sunset still looked beautiful, even with the destroyed city that formed the horizon. The glowing orange skyline was one of the few pleasures the world had left for him.

As the last of the day's light filtered away through the still burning city, Alex's eyes fell to the corpses roaming below him. He watched them wander into open doorways as more wandered out. Through the whiskey induced haze, he felt a twinge of sympathy for the corpses now that they posed less of a threat. He felt their pointless, unending hunger. Their moans sounded more painful now when he really listened.

He took another sip of whiskey. He had never drank so much for so many days straight. He didn't even like drinking, but when he attempted to fool everyone into thinking he was "normal" he would have a few beers with them. Now he had stayed functionally drunk on hard liquor for the fast few days and his body was screaming at him for it. He woke every morning with a headache, but was grabbing the bottle by midday.

The liquor had made it easier for him to accept that the people he killed were not the people he knew. That it was him or them. He was protecting Morgan. It was this justification that worked in his mind because no matter how many times he told himself that these people were dead, when he watched them from the roof, he saw a glimmer of life.

They moved. He took another sip.

The world outside felt much farther away when he was drunk and the world inside appeared so much safer. Safe enough to cry. Safe enough to be scared.

"What are you doing?" Morgan asked from behind, startling him.

Alex turned around in one of the two kitchen chairs he had dragged up to the roof and saw her climbing up the fire escape ladder.

He wiped the tear forming by his eye and said, "Nothing. Just watching the sun go down. I like watching the automatic streetlights turn on. I wonder how much longer they'll last? Even the back-up generators have to run out sometime…"

She sat down next to him, propping her feet up on the edge of the building. She held a can of beer in her hand and took a loud sip. Alex reached down and grabbed his bottle, taking his own sip.

After an endlessly long moment of silence, Morgan finally said, "I feel really stupid."

Alex turned, surprised at the random comment and asked, "What? Why?"

AFTER LIFE

Morgan let out a sigh, still unsure if she should even be talking about what was on her mind. The subject felt so foolish now that she was outside and faced with the world that surrounded them.

"Before I called you, before all of this, before Christopher had left for California... we got into this, like, huge fight. I mean big. We were screaming at each other, which we rarely did. He left the house and I told him I hated him and I really wasn't sure he was going to come back." She took a sip of her beer and shook her head, revealing she understood what she felt was nonsense. "I seriously felt like my life was over. We had dated for so long, you know? He was all I knew. Or thought I knew. And I watched him walk out the door and I felt like that was it. That was all I had. My life just walked out the door." She was immediately embarrassed by her vulnerability. She wished she could suck her words back into her mouth and go on pretending she was strong.

"I'm sure he knew you didn't mean it." Alex tried to be her friend, keeping his responses unbiased. "Everyone fights. Especially couples."

"Yeah, but Alex. That's not the point. I mean look around. I was worried about a boy not being around me. I even called you just because, I mean, I know this is going to sound selfish, or whatever, but I just wanted to know that someone was still going to be in my life. I wanted to know if he left me that at least you would still be there." She shook her head in frustration. "Now the dead are walking the earth and I can't go outside, or they might eat me!"

Alex couldn't help but laugh a bit as he said, "Okay, I see what you're saying."

"I just feel so dumb for all the things I took for granted and all the things I put too much importance on. I mean, I'm not saying Christopher wasn't... *isn't* important. I just... compared to what might have happened to him I would give anything to have us just broken up. At least I would know he was still in the world. Still happy. I just can't believe... I mean, the way I used to think. It seems so foreign to me. It feels wrong in this world. Just a couple weeks and everything is so different."

"No, I've been thinking about that, too. But like, we can't beat ourselves up over having a different life before. It was a different world. Just because in hindsight things don't appear the same, it doesn't make our old views any less valid."

Morgan shook her head, hesitant to share what came next. "I'm just can't stop thinking about Christopher. I just wish I knew what happened. One way or another." She let her head fall into her hands, covering her face. "I feel horrible. I feel like it would be better to know he was dead than to not know." She closed her eyes tight, summoning the power to hold back her tears.

Alex became uncomfortable, trying to call upon every ounce of maturity and sobriety in order to help her. "I feel like that about a lot of people."

"I wonder if he got on the plane before... or, like, if he's wandering around as... as one of those things."

Alex's head swished back and forth as he lifted the bottle of whiskey. He wished he wasn't so drunk. He wanted to give Morgan advice that would set her mind at ease, but could think of nothing. His thoughts swirled from one thought to the next. He set the bottle down without drinking.

As he stared out across the city he focused his mind and said, "Ya know, I sit up here on the roof, and I sit here right, and I think. I try to think about how to save us. What to do so we can be okay. Where to go to be safe, and I..." His voice trailed off, like he lost his breath. Alex readjusted how he was sitting and rested his head in his hands, bracing his elbows on his legs. "I don't know what to do Morgan," he finally said, his voice mixed with a whimper. "I don't know what to do."

"It's okay, Alex." She smiled softly, resting her hand on his back. "We have enough food to last quite a while. We have time to figure it out. We can figure this out together."

He looked into her eyes, hoping what she said was true.

"Alex, you don't have to save me."

He leaned over and he hugged her. He hugged her like he only did when she was leaving a party. When everyone else was hugging her goodbye and it wouldn't be out of the ordinary. He stood in line until it was his turn to wish her goodbye and tried to quietly inhale her perfume, so that he could memorize the smell.

"We should start a fire," Morgan said as she pulled away. They had constructed a makeshift grill on the roof so they could heat up their cans of food.

"Sounds good, we could have some of that soup we found," Alex said, his stomach growling at the thought.

"Okay." Morgan smiled as she crushed her empty beer can under her foot. She looked past him, trying to see how much was left in his bottle. "Do you need something to drink?"

Alex shook his head, knowing he couldn't drink anymore. The food would help him sober up and then maybe he could help Morgan with her problem. She had made him feel better and he had nothing to offer her but his own problems.

His guilt was infinite.

He decided then that he wouldn't drink until this was over. He made a mental promise to himself. A silent contract that he would keep his head clear.

For her.

"Okay I'll crawl down and get the soup," Morgan said. "I need another beer anyways."

Alex just nodded silently, smiling at her. He stood up, wobbling a bit as his equilibrium adjusted, and then walked over to two plastic storage bins that they had been filling with burnable wood. The bins had kept the wood dry and the two bins held more than enough. Most of the wood they found was furniture of some kind, which had been treated with so many chemicals that neither of them were comfortable cooking food over it.

He wondered to himself how long they would resist burning it. He found himself imagining more and more severe situations as the days went on. Wondering how far they could be pushed. He shook his head, trying to push away the thought or reckless survival.

After Alex had soaked the wood in lighter fluid, the flames grew easily. He watched the wood burn away, crackling from black to orange as the light in the sky completely disappeared. The streetlights flickered tonight, showing the signs of failure.

As Morgan climbed back up the ladder, Alex pointed out the surrounding streets. The buildings were dark and could only be seen in the glittering streetlights that were now slowly losing their power. The effect turned the city into a twinkling blanket of black, surrounding them completely.

"It's actually beautiful," Morgan said, staring into the flashing darkness.

They moved their chairs closer to the fire and watched the lights die out little by little, long into the evening, until they were completely enclosed in blackness. The fire they warmed their soup upon, felt like the only light in the world.

AFTER LIFE

Day 14

2:17 pm

On the rooftop Alex looked out over the entire city. The largest buildings were menacing in their emptiness, papers still blowing out their broken windows. Homemade signs that read: *Still Alive!* and *S.O.S.* blew in the wind, attached to poles on the rooftops of the surrounding apartment buildings. Most were shredded, or stained in blood. He wondered how many were still accurate.

He no longer heard the rattle of automatic gunfire, or explosions in the distance to give him hope the military was on their way. It had all happened so quickly. The world had fallen in days. Humanity, society, all its defenses, and trappings took less than two weeks to crumble.

He looked at the sky and could see the twinkle of the sun trying to break through the clouds. More of the gray clumps swooped in, covering its warm rays.

Gunshots rang out right below where Alex was standing, making his heart leap. He looked over the ledge and he saw three men coming out of a doorway, firing at a grouping of corpses running toward them in the alleyway. The three men looked like they were trying to sneak through the building next door, but had been spotted by the corpses in the street.

"Hey!" Alex screamed out over the oceanic roar of moans and the ringing fire of guns. "Run to the back! Get to the fire escape!"

One of the men looked up at him and Alex thrust his arms in a pointing motion toward the back of the building. Alex spun around, dashing across the rooftop, and then started his climb down the fire escape. The gunshots continued ringing out, and Alex saw through the bars of the fire escape the three men run around the building. One was shooting in front and the other two were shooting behind them.

Morgan yelled out the window as Alex ran past, "What is going on? Who's shooting?"

"Survivors! I gotta help!" Alex yelled back as he continued down the ladder, ignoring Morgan's protests.

He dropped to the bottom of the fire escape and unhooked the ladder. The metal beams dropped down, slamming into the pavement below. Corpses came bursting out of the alleyway, running at their top speed toward the three men.

The older man who was dressed in a police uniform and obviously a skilled marksman, unloaded bullets from his pistol with a steady aim, landing head shots with every shot. His younger companion, who wore a baseball cap and t-shirt, jumped onto the ladder and started climbing up to where Alex stood on the bottom platform.

The officer and the middle-aged man in a torn sport coat continued unloading rounds, back to back at the base of the ladder. The corpses ran out of both alleyways now, getting closer and closer with their waves of numbers. Finally, the officer spun around and started climbing the ladder. As the officer made his way to the top of the ladder his leg was grabbed onto by a corpse, fingernails digging into his leg. The man still on the ground twirled around, firing his pistol into the face of the corpse who clung to his companion. Unfortunately, when he turned to help, it gave the corpses he had been firing at the moment they needed to reach him, tackling him to the ground in a violent wave of bodies.

The younger man in the baseball cap yelled out, "Adam!" as the man below was torn apart, the mindless corpses digging into his organs.

The officer grimaced before he kicked his foot out, slamming it into the metal latch that held the ladder to the fire escape. With two more swift kicks, the ladder fell, leaving the parking lot behind the apartment building swarming with undead.

The younger man who looked about the same age as Alex, gasped for breath as he put his hand on the officer. The cop, who was in his early forties, continued staring down at the corpses who gorged themselves on the body of the man in the sport coat. Both men carried packs full of supplies, and the officer had a shotgun slung over one shoulder.

"Alex!" Morgan's voice yelled from above them. "What is going on?"

"It's okay!" He yelled back. "We're coming up!" Alex tried to explain, unsure of what to say. "That's Morgan. My friend. We've been hiding here."

He realized that Morgan was one of the only people he had talked to since the outbreak. Conversations had always been different with her than with "normal" people and the outbreak had only compounded that feeling. He now felt awkward around the living.

"The police aren't coming here to rescue us. Are you?" Alex asked the silent officer, already fearing the answer.

"No." The officer answered so quietly it was hard to hear him. He was still staring at the bodies below him. "Dammit," he said, watching the zombies tear apart his companion. "He had one of our guns."

"Where were you going?" Alex found himself yelling over the excited moans of the mob below.

"We don't know. The last we heard there was a FEMA camp in Hudson, but I don't know if we can count on anything right now," the younger man answered. "We've just been moving from building to building, looking for food or... anything to help us. Everywhere we go it's just... it's just full of..."

"I don't think the camps are still around. I know for sure some of them were compromised." Alex looked up at the apartment window. "We're going to try to stay here. Wait for help. We have food and-"

The officer finally turned toward Alex and asked, bluntly, "Is your building secure?"

"No. I mean sort of." Alex pointed up to the higher levels. "We just have a few apartments blocked off-"

"Is it just the two of you in there?" The cop cut off Alex's explanation, wiping the sweat off his forehead. He was barely listening.

"Yeah. Well my neighbor and his daughter are still alive, but I don't know about anyone else. I haven't heard anyone else." Alex held out his hand. "My name is Alex."

The officer stepped up to Alex. He had a few days stubble covering his square jaw and his face was covered in grime that matched his oily black crew cut. In a gravelly voice he said, "I'm Officer Frank Dallas and this is Ethan Cooper."

Ethan had a smooth skinny face and a nearly translucent reddish-blond hair that hung in curls from underneath his cap. He nodded when introduced and said, "It's really nice to-"

Frank gritted his teeth, cutting into Ethan's introduction. "Do you have any water?"

Alex shook his head. "Not much, the plumbing stopped working awhile ago, but we found plenty of canned soda and beer."

"We would appreciate it," Ethan said, grabbing onto the ladder behind Alex.

When they climbed in the window, Alex yelled out in a sarcastic tone, "Honey, I brought home company."

Morgan stuck her head in the room and jumped a bit when she saw the men carrying guns. "Alex! What's… what's going on?"

Alex held up his hands. "It's okay, I saw these guys from the roof. They're trying to get out of the city."

After some brief introductions, Ethan assured Morgan, "Your boyfriend may have saved our lives down there. We owe him."

Alex took only a moment to notice how it felt to be called Morgan's boyfriend. He did not correct the young man.

"Oh," Morgan said, forcing a smile. "Thanks guys. Um, you can set your stuff down in the living room."

The men nodded at Morgan as they stepped passed her and into the living room. Alex watched them lean a shotgun against the couch and start taking off their backpacks.

"Alex?" Morgan asked in a hush tone, "Are you sure this is a good idea?"

"I didn't know what to do. I mean-"

Morgan shrugged her shoulders. "I know, it's just… forget it. You did the right thing. I'm proud of you."

He leaned in and hugged her. Only inches away from her ear, he said quietly, "Don't worry. Everything will be fine."

She sunk into his shoulder, allowing herself to believe his confidence.

Day 14

6:39 pm

Cases of soda and beer sat next to the refrigerator, most of them only half full. Frank thanked Alex when he offered both the men cans of room temperature soda. Both men gulped down the sugary drinks, obviously pushing the limits of their thirst.
"Thank you Alex," Ethan said, gasping for breath when he finished swallowing. "We've haven't had anything to drink for two days."
"Where did you guys come from?" Morgan asked, sitting on the floor next to Alex.
"We were at that bank a couple blocks away," Ethan explained, pointing north. "We thought we would be safe but-"
"We *were* safe," Frank said, frowning as he finished the can of soda. "But banks don't have much for food."
"Well, you guys are lucky you found each other. Safety in numbers," Morgan said, smiling weakly.

AFTER LIFE

Frank huffed sarcastically, letting himself smile darkly at Ethan.

"I was..." Ethan started explaining bashfully. "I was in the back of the squad car when he got the call that-"

Frank cut him off again. "The bank's alarm was set off when one of these... one of these-"

"Zombies," Alex offered.

Ethan's eyes perked up. "That's what *I've* been calling them! I've been trying to tell him-"

"Yeah kid," Frank shook his head, rubbing his eyes. "You can call these sons-a-bitches whatever you want. It don't matter. They'll kill you the same either way."

"What were you arrested for?" Morgan said, feigning passive curiosity and trying to change the subject.

"I was... it was stupid." Ethan looked at the floor, ashamed.

Frank looked at him through steely cold eyes. "Our friend here was selling drugs."

"It was just weed."

"Weed is a drug, dumbass." Frank's expression did not change.

"Look, it was stupid." Ethan was trying to explain. "I'm done with it. I-"

"You're done with it?" Frank laughed to himself. "I don't think you have much of a choice."

"Yeah, well-" Ethan started, before Frank held up his hand to stop him.

"Listen, I trusted you enough to give you a gun, didn't I?" Frank looked to the window that the moans of the dead emanated from. "Besides, we've got more important things to worry about now."

"Are there still people in the bank?" Alex asked. The tension in the room made him feel uncomfortable.

"No," Frank answered.

"They… they came with us," Ethan explained. "We were making our way through the buildings. Trying to keep off the streets. But-"

"They died. Just like everyone else," Frank finished.

"I'm sorry," Morgan said.

The group sat in silence for a few moments, unsure of how to react next. The thoughts of all the people they had seen die in the last few days came flooding into their minds. Even the ones that had died a second time.

"Did you search any other apartments?" Frank asked, finally breaking the quiet.

"A few. Just the ones we could reach from the fire escape that weren't…" Alex struggled with his words. "Some of the apartments just had too many of those *things*."

"Hey man," Ethan said, smiling, "Don't be embarrassed. We're all scared. We spent most of today running."

Morgan smiled. "We found a lot of food. With the water not working, stuff to drink is going to be the hardest to come by."

"I need to use the bathroom," Ethan said, standing up and looking around.

Alex pointed toward his bedroom window. "Just go out on the fire escape and climb to the roof. We go off the opposite side of the building. "

Ethan shrugged reluctantly and walked into the bedroom.

"We should clear out the building. Scavenge any supplies we can use. We might be here awhile," Frank said. His voice was scratchy and serious.

"There's a lot of those things in the hallways. I don't know how they managed to get upstairs. The doors on the stairwell lock automatically when they close."

"The street in front of the building was thick with them." Frank rubbed his chin, thinking. "I'm sure it's worse closer to ground level. We could at least clear out this floor."

"I don't know," Morgan said, not making eye contact. "We've been killing those things just to get food and water. As long as we have supplies I don't know if it's worth risking. I mean, we've had some pretty close calls."

"We've haven't had guns though," Alex said. Morgan didn't look at him.

"We don't have a lot of ammunition, but we have enough," Frank said, patting the backpack next to him. "I started targeting other cops who were infected and took their ammo."

Alex smiled weakly at him, unsettled by the man's coldness, but simultaneously impressed by his strategy.

Ethan came back in the window. "I can help. I've been getting good with that pistol. You gotta hit these things in the head if you wanna take them down. They don't even feel it anywhere else."

Alex looked at Morgan, seeing the visible worry on her face. He shrugged his shoulders, physically asking her what she thought.

It looked physically taxing for her to agree with the plan. "I guess... I guess we should. We can't all stay in this apartment."

"We can wait till tomorrow," Frank said. "We only have a few hours of daylight left. Alex, you can use the shotgun. Have you ever shot a gun before?"

"Yeah," Alex began. "My dad is a-"

"Whoa, whoa," Morgan's face went white and she held up her hands. "You aren't going with them. We're perfectly safe right here. If you guys want to go searching around-"

"Morgan," Alex stopped her..

"No, no, it's fine," Ethan said. "Right Frank? We can handle things ourselves."

Frank glared at Morgan through his squinted eyes, "Yeah, fine." Frank stood, wiping the smeared grime off his face with his own shirt. "I need some sleep."

"You can sleep in the bedroom," Alex said. He saw Morgan begin to speak up and cut her off. "We're going to be up for awhile so we can stay out here tonight."

Frank said nothing and walked into the bedroom, unbuttoning his shirt.

"He's seen a lot in the last couple weeks," Ethan said, trying to apologize for Frank's attitude.

"We all have," Morgan said matter-of-factly as she walked into the kitchen. "I'm going to make something to eat."

Alex watched her walk away, wishing he had the time to comfort her. Wishing he could make her feel safe again. He could almost see her building back up the wall that she had only begun to let down for him.

"You're lucky, man," Ethan said as he took off his cap and ran his fingers through his greasy hair. "She really cares about you. You can see it. The way she looks at you."

"We care about each other," Alex said, smiling. "I don't know if I could deal with this without her. She's kept me sane."

"Hope."

"What?" Alex asked.

"We all need hope. It's what keeps us going."

Alex nodded. "It's getting rare."

AFTER LIFE

Day 15

8:49 am

Morgan cringed when she saw Frank showing Alex how to load the shotgun. Alex promised her it was only for protection and that he wouldn't leave the apartment. She knew it made logical sense that they would be better off with an entire floor to occupy, and she looked forward to having the apartment to themselves again, but her stomach still felt uneasy.

She remembered that she hadn't had to worry about updating her website in two weeks, and was able to spend entire days hanging out with her best friend. The endless conversation and stories were only broken up by adrenalin filled adventures into other peoples homes. She denied the fact that she was enjoying this new life every day. It felt wrong to be happy about anything now.

Frank looked at his watch and set his hand on the doorknob, nodding at Alex who gripped the shotgun in both hands.

Morgan squeezed the button on the walkie-talkie saying, "Ethan, Frank is about to go into the hallway. You ready?"

The voice of Ethan, who had crawled into an apartment on the other side of the building, came over the walkie-talkie Morgan held and the one clipped to Frank's belt. "I copy. Opening the door... now."

Two doors flung open simultaneously and the hallway was filled with crossfire. The infected bodies wandering through the third floor were torn apart by bullets and the building thundered with the sounds of gunfire. Heads exploded in a spray of dead flesh and the infected bodies fell to the floor.

"Hallway is clear," Ethan said as he crouched down on one knee. "I'm covering the doors."

Frank made his way to the stairwell door and saw a headless body slumped over the top step, keeping the door propped open. Corpses wandered up the stairs slowly, making their way into the upper levels. Frank stepped forward, firing at the few corpses that started running up the stairs when they saw him. He knelt down and shoved the corpse on the floor down the steps, then stepped back and watched the large metal door slam shut, locking as it did.

Frank stepped over one of the fallen bodies in the hallway and made his way toward the first apartment door.

"I'm entering 303," he said into the walkie-talkie as he placed his hand on the doorknob. He jiggled the handle and found it locked.

"If anyone is in there, open the door! I'm a police officer!" Frank spoke with authority, but tried his best to not sound hostile.

He waited a few moments and then stepped back. With a swift kick the door came crashing in, landing against a small dresser. Frank pushed the dresser out of the way and raised his pistol, pointing it at the man hunched over on a couch. His trigger finger instinctively started to squeeze when the man turned his face around.

"Ethan, I found the other survivor."

"Copy that," Ethan said through the radio. Frank heard gunshots, then, "Hallway is still secure."

Frank stepped toward the round man who was hunched over in fear, yet still held a look of anger on his face. "Mr. Peterson, where is your daughter?"

Mr. Peterson looked up at the officer with an angry look. "You sons-a-bitches took long enough! I've been sitting here for weeks!"

The large man started to lift himself off the couch before Frank pushed him back into his seat with one hand.

"Stay where you are Mr. Peterson. Where is your daughter? I need to make sure all the survivors are secure."

The bathroom door opened up and Frank spun around, shoving the barrel of his pistol into Emma's face.

"I'm right here," she said weakly, frozen in fear.

Frank dropped the barrel, pointing his gun at the floor. He stepped back toward the front door.

"All known survivors accounted for, Ethan. But, god dammit be careful, there may be more Alex didn't know about." More gunshots rang out.

Emma sat down next to her father on the couch. She looked to her Dad as Frank began to step back in the hallway and asked, "Is he a real cop? Is he here to save us?"

Frank looked back into apartment. "Sorry folks. We're just going to help you clear out the building, make it safer if you want to stay here." Ethan fired again. This time Frank saw two men fall down, only ten yards from his position. "I have to keep moving. We're hoping to have things cleared out in an hour. Maybe more. Just hang tight."

"What?" Mr. Peterson looked enraged. "What kind of plan is that? Just take us back with you."

"We don't have anywhere to 'go back to.' I don't even have a police department anymore. We're all on our own now."

"Who the hell do you think you are?" Mr. Peterson was just spouting random questions now, overtaken by his rage. Down the hall Ethan fired again, this time hitting a dead woman who came crawling out of her apartment.

"Sir, stay in your apartment until we tell you it's safe, or you will be shot." Frank stepped into the hallway and raised his gun. Frank turned his back to the Peterson's apartment and looked down the hall. "Okay Ethan, lets start clearing these apartments."

"Copy that," Ethan said, checking to see how many rounds he had left in his magazine. He was getting better at head shots and was happy to see he still had half a clip.

The first two apartments were empty, but in the third Ethan had to shoot two rounds into a six year old boy who jumped off the top of a bunk-bed at him. The child fell to the floor and stayed there, stunned just long enough for Ethan to release one final round into the child's skull. The young man was shaken by how easy it was becoming. He wanted to stop and mourn what he was just forced to do, but he moved on. He pushed the image from his mind easily and let himself feel the excitement of the violence.

Gunshots rang through the hallway as Frank found more infected nearby. Ethan had lost track of how many reanimated corpses he had killed so far. This floor was nearly empty compared to other buildings they had been in, but the infestation was always thicker on the ground floor. He had killed a lot of these things and he planned on killing a lot more.

A simple sweep and clear, he told himself. *Just like a video game. Just helping the neighbors with some spring cleaning.*

The next apartment's door hung open, connected to the door frame by only one hinge. Daylight barely made its way into the living room through holes in a large blanket hung over the window. Ethan reached to the barrel of his pistol and flipped a switch, turning on the light mounted there. The beam of white light cut through the dusty shadows, revealing the room. Unwashed dishes were piled on the coffee table and dirty clothes nearly covered the floor.

A man snarled in the kitchen, then leapt out at Ethan. Ethan brought up his pistol in time to shove it into the man's wide open mouth. The corpse gnawed on the metal of the barrel before Ethan gathered his wits and pulled the trigger, splattering the man's brains on the wall behind him. The body fell to the ground and Ethan shivered.

A little too close.

Ethan stepped carefully, hearing the crunch of debris under his boot. The living room and kitchen were empty, but the beam of light sliced through the air, landing on the bedroom door. His boots moved slowly and methodically, taking their time.

Scratches ran down the bedroom door, only broken periodically by dents that looked like impacts from a fist. With a slow turn, he found the doorknob locked and took a deep breath.

With a lunge, he slammed into the door with his shoulder. The door went crashing in, falling clean off its hinges. The flashlight on the pistol cut into the dark room and Ethan saw movement, a body jumping off the bed. He fired, hitting the person squarely in the chest. They reeled back, letting out a scream of pain.

Without thinking Ethan fired again and heard the same scream.

The dead don't feel pain.

The realization he had just shot a survivor slapped him in the face. He shined the light of his gun down on the body and saw a dark skinned boy, no older than eighteen, squirming in pain.

"Oh shit man. Oh shit, you shot me," the boy said, holding his bloody shirt.

"Oh fuck. Frank!" Ethan yelled into his walkie-talkie and crouched down next to the bleeding boy. "Frank, I got a problem."

"What is it, Ethan?"

Ethan grabbed a hold of the blanket that covered the window in the bedroom and tore it down. Sunlight poured in, revealing the true state of affairs.

The impossibly skinny body laid on the floor in nothing but boxers and a t-shirt, bleeding onto the floor from two wounds. One was just above his heart, covering his entire shoulder in red blood. The other was in his hip and looked as though the bullet had passed clean through.

"Why the hell did you shoot me, man?" the boy said. His clean-shaven head was covered with sweat and blood.

"Frank," Ethan began into the walkie-talkie. "I... I shot one of the survivors. Oh shit." He started to help the boy lay flat on the floor. "I'm in apartment 308."

There was a pause on the walkie-talkie. Then: "Moving to your position."

Ethan kept repeating, "I'm sorry, I'm so sorry" until Frank came through the door.

"Ethan, secure the hallway!" Frank said as he holstered his gun and crouched next to the boy. "The last thing we need is one of those corpses sneaking up on us."

Frank leaned down and checked the wound on the boy's chest. "My name is Frank Dallas, what's yours?"

"Omar," the skinny boy said, a drop of blood forming by his mouth.

"Okay Omar. I'm a police officer, but before that I was a captain in the United States Army. I served two tours of duty in Iraq. I had a lot of friends get shot Omar, and I had to deal with a lot of field wounds."

"Field wound?" Omar coughed. "Your partner shot me while I was sleeping, dude!"

AFTER LIFE

Frank flipped out his utility knife and started cutting Omar's t-shirt off. The knife sliced through the moist, bloody cloth easily, and the shirt fell away, exposing the wound completely.

"Omar, do you have any alcohol in the house?"

Omar squinted his eyes in pain, groaning out his answer, "I don't know. I've been in this room for... for days. My dad always had vodka on top of the fridge, but my dad was the one I was hiding from."

"What about tweezers?"

Omar groaned at the thought. "I think... I think there's some in the bathroom."

Frank got up and walked into the filthy kitchen, stepping over the body of Omar's father. The room looked like a murder scene from a movie. Blood was sprayed across everything in thin streams, ending in large stains of blood, sometimes still accompanied by hunks of human meat.

Frank had seen worse, but was still taken aback by the gross display. He scanned the top of the fridge and found a bottle of half empty vodka.

The bathroom was nearly untouched, looking as it did before the infection. It took him longer to find the tweezers, digging through the many drawers next to the sink.

"Now, I need you to lie perfectly still," Frank said as he walked back into the bedroom. Unscrewing the cap he poured the alcohol over the wound. He leaned in close to Omar's chest, trying to peer inside the entry wound.

"It's not bad, Omar. You're lucky."

"I don't feel lucky."

"I can see the bullet. It looks like it bounced off your collar bone, but didn't break it." Frank smiled into Omar's face, trying to keep his spirits up. "You've got strong bones, buddy!"

Omar gave him a weak smile and more blood trickled out of his mouth.

"Now," Frank said, his face becoming serious. "This may hurt a bit."

Morgan and Alex sat in their living room, their bodies jumping every time a gunshot went off. The walkie-talkie sat in the middle of the coffee table, letting them listen to everything that was happening.

A voice finally spoke from the box. "Alex! Morgan!"

Morgan grabbed the walkie-talkie and held down the talk button. "We're here!"

"We almost have your floor clear, but I need to get Omar here somewhere we can keep him flat and change his bandages. Make sure to clear some room and get some clean cloth ready for him."

Morgan looked at Alex and he nodded, looking surprised she would ask his approval for something like that.

"Okay, we will right away." Morgan tried to use a tone to assure Frank, and then asked, "Is he going to be okay?"

There was a long silence before Frank answered back in a whisper: "I don't know."

Hearing there was another survivor in the apartment alone, locked in his bedroom for weeks, made Morgan feel horrible for her selfishness and hoarding. Branching out and helping other survivors was the right thing to do. And while danger may be more present in her life after that day, overall she felt better about the new direction.

Alex opened his apartment door slowly, gripping the shotgun tightly, still expecting a dead person to leap out at him from the hallway. Ethan knelt outside the door, his pistol stretched out in front of him. He scanned back and forth, trying to watch both directions, but said nothing.

Less than a minute later, Frank came shuffling backwards into the apartment, dragging the wounded Omar on a sheet behind him. He set him down gently on the kitchen floor.

"Cut up whatever clean cloth you can find. Keep his bandage clean and keep pressure on it." Frank spoke to Morgan, then slung his shotgun off his shoulder and stepped behind Ethan in the hallway.

"Let's move, Ethan. I want to finish this."

"But Frank." Ethan took one hand off his pistol, lowering it, and turned his head toward Omar. "Should I-"

Frank grabbed Ethan's face by his jaw, turning it so he was looking into Frank's eyes.

"I want to finish this."

The men moved away from the door and Alex heard gunshots only moments later.

Alex and Morgan took care of Omar, who was now fast asleep and had finally stopped bleeding. They did this while listening to the gunfire that echoed down the hall and the screams of commands that emanated from the walkie-talkie. They spoke very little, consumed with their own anxiety and their own anticipation for the men to be done.

Frank let out a heavy breath as the last corpse in the last apartment fell to the ground. "That's all we can do Ethan. We'll use all our ammo if we try to clear another floor." He looked at Ethan, who stared at the floor, unresponsive.

Frank frowned, asking, "What is it?"

Ethan shook his head. "I shot that kid. I mean, I was trying to help and I-"

Frank cringed. He hated this part of his job. It was hard enough for him to keep his own emotional armor built up, he didn't want to have to help Ethan do the same.

Frank gritted his teeth and leaned in close to Ethan. "Listen, I asked you... we all asked you to shoot these people. We asked you to shoot almost everything in this building. Your actions may not have been perfect, but you still did good. If that boy up there dies, you cannot let his one death outweigh all of the deaths that you wanted to cause. The good deaths."

Frank looked at Ethan, knowing the young, overly-sensitive man didn't understand his logic. He would need to harden him more if he was going to make him an effective partner. He grabbed his walkie-talkie and called it in.

"Looks like we're done here, folks. We have the floor."

AFTER LIFE

Day 15

10:59 am

Mr. Peterson stood in the corner of the room, his thick, hairy arms crossed over his sweaty chest. He watched his daughter Emma reapplying the bandage to the boy on the ground. For a moment, a feeling somewhat like pride came over him. It lasted for only a moment.

"Emma," Mr. Peterson said under his breath. "Get over here. Let somebody else take care of him."

Emma looked up at her father, surprised. When she saw the look on her father's face she stood up and handed the cloth to Ethan, keeping her eyes on the floor. She slowly walked over and stood next to her father.

Only Alex understood why Mr. Peterson wouldn't want his light skinned daughter to help the dark skinned boy. Alex caught himself wondering why someone like Mr. Peterson was spared.

"Have any of you heard from family or anything?" Morgan asked, handing out cans of soda to everyone.

"I was in contact with the station up until 2 days ago," Frank said, popping open a can of root beer. "I never heard from my wife."

"My cousin called me when this all started happening," Mr. Peterson said. "But he was going to the FEMA camp in Hudson. I doubt he's still alive."

"My Dad e-mailed me from Wisconsin," Alex offered to the conversation. "He said he was fine. That was about a week ago. There aren't many people around where he lives, so I'm still hopeful."

Eyes darted around the room, everyone waiting for someone else to continue the list, but no one else spoke. The room was depressingly quiet. The murmur of the dead outside filled the emptiness.

"That goddamn noise they make is going to drive me insane," Mr. Peterson yelled out the window, as if passive-aggressively asking the zombies to be quiet.

"It's become like white noise to me," Morgan said, staring off into space. "I don't even hear it anymore." Just as quickly, her eyes snapped back to reality and she took a deep breath.

"We need to talk about what we do next," Frank said, stepping forward and hooking his thumbs on his belt. "First of all, we need to stay away from that blood until we figure out a way to clean it up." Frank sipped his soda, thinking. "We need to get rid of those bodies before they rot any worse."

"I have a good pair of gloves," Alex said. "I can start searching the apartments for tools, and gloves, and... what? Bleach?"

"Yeah." Morgan shrugged, unsure. "Any cleaning supplies would be good."

Alex stood up to start digging in his closet for his gloves.

Mr. Peterson frowned. "So we're just gonna start stealing from our neighbors?"

Frank stepped forward as soon as Mr. Peterson started talking. By the time he had finished his question, Frank was in his face. "We are going to do whatever it takes to survive."

Mr. Peterson huffed out a breath from underneath his mustache and leaned against the wall. Looking back and forth for someone to take his side.

No one did.

Alex slipped his gloves on and stepped into the hallway. "I'll let you know if I find anything."

Alex heard the group start to take stock of what food they had as he walked down the hallway, trying to reassure himself that Frank and Ethan had killed all the corpses.

The rotting bodies slumped against the wall, crumpled heaps underneath splatters of blood filled with bullet holes that smeared down to the spot they lay. The corpses were almost unrecognizable now, the skin mottled and blue with greenish pustules covering their bodies. Bones jutted out from torn away flesh. Organs hung from the gaping holes, draped across the floor in a bloody mess. The inside of the bodies looked hollow now, like they were liquefying from the inside.

He stepped carefully, keeping himself away from the walls and stepping over the pools of blood. He could not keep his eyes off each body he passed though, assuming every one would leap up at him at any moment.

Dead just isn't what it used to be.

The first few apartments had plenty of food and clean clothes, which the group would need very badly with no water to clean with. But soon he began finding half full bottles of bleach under people's bathroom sinks, and even a few flashlights, which would make the evenings a little easier for everyone.

In the last apartment he found an old boom-box that was meant for compact discs, but had a radio as well. He hit the power button and smiled as the batteries turned the system on.

Static erupted from the speakers and Alex swirled the dial up, passing through the stations. When he heard nothing, he spun the dial down, slowly searching for any noise patterns. Nothing came from the speakers. He hit the power button and picked it up by its handle, carrying two bottles of bleach under the other arm and gripping a plastic bag full of gloves and sponges.

The group started breaking into two groups when Alex returned. Some became body disposers, tasked with hauling the bodies to the window at the end of the hallway and tossing them out. The other group became blood removers, soaking the blood out of the hallway floor and doing what they could to wipe down the blood splattered on the walls.

By late afternoon, all the bodies had been removed and even Omar had woken up. The group's morale was obviously higher, and while Morgan had taken care of Omar that afternoon, she had also made dinner from canned fruits and bagels.

The meal was prepared. Set out on plates and bowls as everyone returned to the clean apartment, dropping their exterior clothes out in the hallway. Sitting around in shorts and t-shirts, with a cool breeze finally blowing in after the sweltering heat of the day, the group devoured the meal. They even managed to laugh a few times while they ate.

When the meal was done, Ethan started to put his dirty clothes back on.

Alex looked out into the hallway as he was carrying dishes into the kitchen and asked, "Going somewhere?"

"Yeah, there's some bleach left and I want to see if I can get the blood out of that last apartment on the left. It doesn't have much on the floor and it would be nice to not have to share a place with Frank."

"I can understand that." Alex shrugged. "You want some help?"

"If you want to grab the mop." Ethan pointed at the mop in the kitchen. "Most of the blood is on the tile. I'll grab the bleach."

Alex nodded and set the dishes in the kitchen. He wondered, with no way to clean them, if he should just throw them out the window before they start growing mold. He really didn't want to start littering already, so he stacked them neatly next to the unusable sink.

He snatched up the mop and started putting on his jeans that he wore while disposing bodies. Frank followed him down the hall, telling everyone he was ready to call it a night. Alex heard Mr. Peterson start arguing with Emma about staying with Morgan to help take care of Omar.

He said goodnight to Frank just as he reached the last apartment on the left, and heard a loud *THUD*, like something heavy hitting the floor.

"Oh shit!" Ethan yelled out.

Frank and Alex ran into the room, Alex holding up his mop like a weapon. They both looked into the kitchen and saw Ethan laying on the floor, his face and hands covered in blood.

"What happened?" Alex yelled, stepping closer to him, but unwilling to touch him.

"Oh shit. Oh shit, shit, shit!" Ethan said, touching the blood on his face to see how much was there. His hand was bare, the pair of gloves were lying on the counter. "I hadn't even put my gloves on yet. I was walking across the kitchen to open the shade to get some light in here. I slipped on the blood."

Alex and Frank just stared at him with their mouths wide.

"Oh my god, I have it all over me. It's in my mouth!" Ethan started spitting the blood on the floor, and then looked up at Frank and Alex gasping out the words, "What do I do? What do I do?"

Alex stumbled backwards and looked behind him, seeing a clean curtain hanging in front of the window. He ran across the room and ripped the cloth from the rod.

As he handed the curtain to Ethan, he ordered, "Wipe it off. Don't rub your eyes!" He turned toward Frank, suddenly getting a surge of aggressiveness. "Go get a bottle of water. We need to flush his eyes."

Frank hesitated, not moving for a moment, and then pulled out his pistol. "We shouldn't waste the water."

"Oh shit, Alex." Ethan was crying. "What the hell? Am I seriously going to get sick from this?"

Alex watched Ethan whimper as he wiped the blood from his face. It was thick, like blackened crimson syrup, as he smeared it from his smooth cheeks.

"It already got in my mouth," Ethan said before spitting on the floor again.

"Frank! Go get water. We need to flush his eyes." Alex tried to stay calm, but couldn't help screaming.

"It's a virus. It got in my body. I'm going to die, Alex!" Ethan's eyes were gigantic and he spit tears when he screamed.

Frank pointed the pistol at Ethan, saying, "He's right."

Ethan began screaming, cowering away from Frank's pistol. "Please don't kill me!" He continued wiping and spitting. Tears rolled down his face.

"Put your gun away!" Alex screamed, grabbing onto Frank's arm.

Morgan ran into the apartment, Mr. Peterson right behind her. Mr. Peterson stopped at the door, looking into the kitchen and seeing the blood covered Ethan.

"Oh my god, Alex, is he going to-" Morgan grabbed onto his arm, digging her nails in like she did in the diner when they saw their first infected corpse.

"No, we haven't seen anyone change into those things from getting blood on them!" Alex yelled. "We've never seen anyone get sick just from the blood. Nothing happens unless you die!"

Frank looked skeptical. "The folks on the radio were saying it was a virus. Viruses travel through blood."

Alex shook his head. "No. Not all of them. We were only assuming…" His mind wandered to all of the apartments he and Morgan had raided. The splatter of blood from the corpses. The spray of brains. The gore covered bodies they both became accustomed to. He almost spoke out, letting people know he had been exposed to the blood and nothing had happened to *him*.

His own fears kept him silent.

Frank glared at Alex, speaking through his teeth as if Ethan couldn't hear him. "It's too dangerous. We can't let him come back as one of those."

"No, no. Alex is right," Morgan said. "We don't know anything for sure. You can't just shoot him!"

"What do you want to do? Sit around and wait for him to get sick?" Frank yelled, "You want to wait for him to start chewing on you while you sleep? Or infect us all when he sneezes?"

"I am not okay with that!" Mr. Peterson's voice shouted from behind them. He stood listening from the doorway.

"It will be fine, Mr. Peterson." Morgan held up her hand, trying unsuccessfully not to roll her eyes at his outburst.

"It will not be fine!" He yelled, stomping into the room, waving his index finger back and forth in the air. "If that boy is infected, he needs to be outside where he can't infect us! He's one of them now!"

Alex was shocked by the man's attitude. "One of them? We're just speculating on how this works. None of us are doctors, and you want to throw him outside? You just want to kill him because it makes sense in your tiny little mind?"

"I don't want him to infect me, or my daughter!" Mr. Peterson stood close to Alex, trying to stare him down.

"He stays in my apartment," Alex said, not flinching. "If you are that scared of him, you can go ahead and board up the door."

Mr. Peterson's eyes squinted before he huffed out a puff of breath, blowing his mustache hairs out like a walrus. He turned and stormed out of the apartment. Stomping down the hallway, he then slammed his apartment door shut.

Frank glared at Alex, spitting his words out from tight lips. "You're putting yourself in danger."

"When the hell am I *not* in danger?" Alex asked, honestly. "I'm not killing one of the only people I know is still alive. He stays with me. We'll lock the door. Give me a gun. If he changes, then I'll kill him without flinching."

Ethan whimpered at the idea.

Frank ground his teeth together, before finally holstering his pistol and saying, "You don't get a gun. I've lost too many to people who flinched." Frank began walking out of the apartment, but stopped at the doorway. "You need to accept the fact that the same rules as before don't apply anymore, Alex. The quicker you change with the world, the safer you'll be." He turned his head, locking his squinty eyes with Alex. "It's adaptation." He walked out the door.

Alex looked at Ethan who was blinking his eyes to try to get the last of the blood out of them. He tried to offer words of comfort to Ethan. "There are flesh eating corpses outside, and I still find that guy scary."

Ethan managed to let out a single chuckle. "Thank you, Alex. Thank you so much."

AFTER LIFE

Day 17

12:31 pm

Ethan had remained unchanged for over 24 hours. Alex swore to everyone outside the apartment that this was sufficient evidence he would be fine, but no one agreed. Deep down, even Alex knew he might be wrong, and he was worried he would be risking everyone's lives by opening the door.

Once the door had been locked and he realized he had sealed himself off from Morgan, doubts began to creep into his mind. He kept his baseball bat near, but tried not to treat Ethan any different.

Morgan had assured him that whatever this virus was, it wasn't airborne. They had spent enough time with the windows open and on the roof, to have contracted something. If it was in the air, they would all be sick.

Alex knew that he had gotten blood on himself in the past, but paranoia told him he never had the amount that Ethan had gotten on himself. He had never gotten it in his mouth, or his eyes. He had always covered any scratches or open wounds. He reminded himself that no one acted any different until they were dead. The virus was only affecting people once they died.

Maybe the virus didn't kill them.

Maybe the carriers had to do the killing.

He recited these ideas over and over in his head, but he still hadn't been able to sleep yet. His mind grew foggy with exhaustion. His vision was blurred and his thoughts dulled with slowness.

"You okay?" Ethan asked.

"I'm fine," Alex said, stretching his back and opening his eyes wide.

"This is getting ridiculous," Ethan complained. "I'm obviously not sick."

"You can't blame them, Ethan. They're worried. The news kept using the word 'virus.' Even if it was a buzzword, it ended up adding context to something we knew nothing about."

"But it's so obviously not a virus. You said it yourself: Zombies!"

"Right, well, what does that mean though?"

"It means it's the end of the world, man!" Ethan was visibly excited, nearly flabbergasted that Alex didn't already think the same way. "God's pissed off and we're paying for it."

Alex hesitated at even beginning the conversation. "You think God did this?"

"Hey listen, I'm not some bible-thumping, right-wing type, but it's sort of hard to ignore the signs."

"I don't remember zombies in the bible."

Ethan frowned. "I'm pretty sure they're in there."

"I don't know…" Alex let his argument trail off, seeing no point. Ethan was obviously going to believe what he wanted to believe.

AFTER LIFE

"It totally makes sense if you think about it. We've been pissing God off for a long time now. It makes sense that he would do something like this."

Alex tried not to show his annoyance with the idea. He may not have been going to church every Sunday, but he definitely believed in a higher power. When he heard people talk about religion like this it scared him. People who feel that somehow they have a special understanding of God and are more than willing to talk for him.

"Do you think it hurts? Do you think they can feel anything?"

Alex let out a heavy sigh, becoming frustrated with the constant topic. "I don't think those things feel anything. Pain, sympathy, happiness, or sadness. Those things aren't people anymore, Ethan."

Ethan nodded, appearing to understand and agree. "I just wonder. When we die, when we change, what will it be like?"

"*If* we die, it wouldn't matter," Alex said plainly. "We'd be dead."

"I know!" Ethan assured him. "I just wonder..."

Alex shook his head in frustration. Ethan was the same age as him, but acted years younger. It felt like Ethan was always asking the dumbest questions, always worried about the most insignificant things. These things were becoming more than annoyances in the too-small-of-a-room.

Ethan let a natural pause happen as he formed how to arrange his words. "I can't believe you stood up for me, Alex. I'm not sure I can thank you enough times."

Alex held up his hand. "Seriously, I'm just doing what I thought was right. I'm not going to just let us start shooting each other."

"Yeah but," Ethan said, his eyes squinting, "I'm not sure I trust everyone here, you know?"

"What? Like who?"

"Frank obviously has issues."

"Yeah, but I can't blame him for having problems dealing with this. There's no right way to deal with this. Like I said: I can't blame them for being suspicious. It only matters what they chose to do in the end."

Ethan hesitated before asking, "Do you think he doesn't trust me because of what I did to Omar?"

"No, Ethan." Alex had seen how guilty Ethan felt about Omar, but Alex was too tired to reassure his self confidence for him. "That was an accident. This is totally unrelated. Besides, Omar will be okay."

"Okay fine, but that Peterson guy. He's obviously messed up."

Alex smirked. "Well, you might be right on that one."

Both of them started laughing, inebriated from a lack of sleep. Alex tried to push the thoughts of annoyance with Ethan out of his head. He reminded himself he was simply becoming agitated because he was tired, and they had been in the same room for so long. Alex wondered if eventually everyone would get on his nerves.

Alex stood up and walked over to the kitchen counter where the boom-box sat. He pushed in on the power button and started turning the knob, slowing roaming through the static.

"Still searching?" Ethan called out, trying to sound sincere, afraid he would sound like he was mocking Alex's quest.

"Yeah," he yelled into the living room. "I just… if I had something to offer people. Something to let them know there were other people. That somebody was organized."

"Wouldn't that be incredible? Maybe God let some of us live. Like Noah. Maybe that's what this is!" Ethan yelled his excitement. "It's just a flood!"

Alex shrugged his shoulders, completely unwilling to approach any conflict.

I'm so tired.

"Maybe. Maybe your right. I don't know. I just can't imagine we're the only group who survived. Odds are, someone is out there." His finger finished the dial spin and he switched over to AM, rolling it back up.

"I'm sure someone is alive," Ethan agreed. "I mean. I don't *feel* special, ya know?"

As Alex hit the power button on the radio, with no luck finding anything other than static, the apartment door burst open. Morgan stood holding the doorknob on the other side and her worried face looked up to meet Alex.

Pulling away from her excited gaze, Alex saw Mr. Peterson standing in the doorway, looking steamed and saying, "This doesn't make me feel any better. It doesn't explain anything! He's just a kid!"

"What's going on?" Alex asked Morgan, who had a giant smile on her face.

"We were talking to Omar and he said-" She tried to catch her breath. "He said his dad never got bitten. His dad had a heart attack because he didn't have his heart medication, and that's when he turned into a zombie! That's when poor Omar locked himself in his room!"

"So his dad wasn't infected!" Ethan yelled.

Alex's eyebrows scrunched up, his brain kicking into overdrive.

"What?" Morgan asked. "I know that look. What are you thinking?"

"I'm not sure it means Omar's dad wasn't infected." Alex sat down on a kitchen chair, holding his head as it throbbed with the desire to sleep. "I think it means we're all infected."

Day 17

3:00 pm

Morgan peeked in the door to the bedroom and saw Alex climbing into bed. He had slipped out of his pants and was only wearing boxer shorts. His body looked skinny, but toned. She had never seen this much of him.

Embarrassed, she stepped away from the door for a couple seconds and then knocked.

"Yeah?" he called out, his voice weak.

"Hey," she said, smiling and walking in. The sheets were now pulled up to his waist, covering his lower half. She sat down on the edge of the bed with a sympathetic look on her face. "Are you okay?"

He rubbed his eyes and rolled over on his side. "Yeah. I just... now my brain won't shut off. I mean, can you imagine if this is real. If we're all going to become one of those things?"

"Alex." Her fingers ran across his head, her fingernails scratching him lightly. "Even if it is true... we're still alive. Nothing is going to happen to us."

"We're going to die eventually. I mean it's inevitable. Someday I'm going to be walking around like one of those things."

"You don't know that."

"But that's what it looks like. I mean, it makes sense."

Morgan couldn't argue with him. None of them knew anything about virology, or biology. No one could argue what they saw with their own eyes.

"I'm just so tired. I wish I could sleep."

Morgan smiled at him, her head tilted to the side and her eyebrows curved slightly as if she were sad.

"I was really proud of what you did."

"What?" Alex's eyes drooped low.

"I was really proud of you. Protecting Ethan like that. You saved his life."

"I don't think I saved his life. I just couldn't let... I mean, that was crazy right?"

"It was."

"People were just ready to flip a switch. They were ready to just-"

"They were trying to protect themselves. And the ones they loved."

"Well no, I get that. I mean, I wanted to protect you, too."

"I know. But you found a way to protect everyone. You figured out a way to do the right thing. Not just the easy thing."

Alex smiled at Morgan, her voice calmed his mind. She had made him feel safe again. Just him and her, alone in the apartment.

Her hand lifted off the bed and rested on his belly. He could feel the warmth of her palm through the sheets.

"I'm so glad you're here," she said.

"I can't imagine dealing with any of this without you, Morgan."

"I thought regular life was hard without you."

He laughed weakly.

"I'm serious," she said.

Alex began to open his mouth when he felt her hand start to slide down the sheet. His eyes locked with hers, a look of surprise running across his face. Her face remained gentle and sympathetic.

Her hand stopped on top of his penis and she grabbed it in her hand, softly.

"Morgan, what are you-" Alex's body stiffened up and his arms moved to stop her.

"Don't," Morgan said, her single finger touching his lips to quiet him. "Let me do this. Please."

His mind flushed with adrenalin and his body began to quiver. He was in a state of shock, trying to piece together what was happening. She laid down next him, her hand stroking him even though he remained soft.

"When you locked yourself in that room, I was so proud of you." Her voice was a whisper, warm breath tickling his ear. "But it made me realize what it would be like without you."

"You don't have to do this," he said, feeling himself become hard in her warm hand.

"I know Alex. I'm doing this because I want to make you feel the way you make me feel."

"You do, Morgan. Every day."

Her hand kept moving and his body began to tingle with sensation.

He wondered if she was doing this because she missed Christopher. Suddenly the act became tainted in his mind and his body rejected the normally good feeling.

AFTER LIFE

"We can't do this," he said, pushing her hand away from. He moved his entire body away from her, his skin aching at the removal of her touch.

"What?" Morgan looked surprised at the turn of events.

"Morgan, I don't know why you're doing this, but you don't know that Christopher is dead. He could still be alive."

Her face scrunched up in a look somewhere between confusion and disgust. "Why would you say that? Why would you say that right *now*?"

"I just-"

"This has nothing to do with Christopher," she said. The spite in her voice stung his ears.

"But I... I mean..."

"No," she said, dropping her head and waving her hand as she stood up from the bed. "I just wanted to be close to you. I haven't felt close to you in years, and I wanted to remind you that you're still alive. That you still have a life to live." She looked away from him. "Maybe I needed to remind myself of that too."

"Morgan, I'm sorry. I just didn't want you to do something and regret it, or-"

She walked toward the door to the bedroom and looked back one last time. "I wouldn't have regretted it," she said, before stepping into the hallway.

Alex sank back into his pillow and looked at the ceiling. His penis was still stiff, lifting the sheet away from his hips. His mind rushed with a million things he should have said. A million different outcomes to the interaction. Yet only one expression stood out in his mind as something he should have said instead, repeating itself over and over as he replayed the event in his mind. One series of words that would forever be etched onto his brain. One phrase was all he wanted to turn back time and say.

I love you.

Day 23

2:55 pm

Alex sat on a stool near the window in the kitchen, turning the dial on the boom-box, passing over station after station of static. This had become his obsessive pastime.

He scratched his face as he turned the dial, itching at the beard that had begun to grow. Some of the men had been using the shaving cream they found to maintain a groomed look, but Alex was losing the will to care.

Ethan still did not show any signs of getting sick. Mr. Peterson pointed out every time Ethan raised his voice, or ate his can of peaches strangely, but the rest of the group had relaxed into the idea that the blood was not infectious. The problem with that answer was that it raised even more questions.

Morgan sat on the floor with Emma, playing a board game with Omar, who was sitting upright now. The three of them got along fairly well and it was obvious Emma had become smitten with Omar.

AFTER LIFE

As Alex watched Emma flirt with the boy, he realized that just two weeks ago, he would have frowned upon their relationship. Emma wasn't even fourteen years old and Omar was nearing his eighteenth birthday.

Now, as he watched the two laughing, he was just glad they had each other. He had realized that taboos from life, before all the death, fell away into absurdity. Hope for even a moment of happiness was all that mattered now.

The heat was rising everyday, making the idea of leaving the windows closed an impossibility. The stink of the undead drifted through the apartment building, sticking to everything it lingered on. Most of the group wore handkerchiefs, or t-shirts over their nose and mouth, some even spraying cologne on the outside as a scent filter.

Alex continued to spin the dial.

Every apartment on the third floor had been looted clean. Every useful item was placed in a single apartment they had converted to a storage area. They had taken stock of every food item and tool. Every piece of clothing and chemical. Every pharmaceutical and bottle of water.

The group estimated they had enough food to last a little over a month, if they ate sparingly. The hard part would be drinking enough water. Including the soda and beer, they only had enough to last two more weeks if they each only drank one can a day. Frank had already begun planning a raid of the second floor.

Alex continued searching the dial.

Morgan stood up and walked over to where Alex was sitting, putting her arm around him and squeezing gently. They hadn't talked about the incident between them since it happened. Alex still felt the need to keep his distance and he let the coldness inside him fester. Morgan had begun to act more like nothing happened every day that passed.

Moments and flashes of how he truly felt would reveal themselves to him, but he pushed the ideas away.

Somehow anger and pain were easier. He could simply give into those emotions. No fighting required.

Morgan turned her head, smiling. "Where are you at?"

"Hmm?" Alex murmured, coming out of his distant thoughts. "Oh, sorry." His mind grasped at what he was just thinking about before his mind turned to her. "I was... I was thinking about everyone. Like Jacob and Liz. Or Mark. Or Kelly. Or my Mom."

Morgan placed her hand behind his head and pulled him close, setting her chin on top of his head as she held him.

"Alex, I don't know what to tell you. We can't know if they're alive, or dead, or-"

Alex let her squeeze him tight one last time and then leaned away from her. "I keep imagining where they were. How each one would react."

"We're never going to know all that."

"I know, I just-"

"You have to hope they are safe, wherever they are," Morgan said as she stared out the window, looking down at the corpses wandering in the streets. "Have you noticed them moving slower?"

"It's the heat I think," Alex mumbled, drifting into the subject change. "The birds have been pecking away at them, too."

Morgan's face looked blank. "I wish they would just rot away. Turn to dust."

He shrugged his shoulders. He had the same thought before, but something was bothering him. "What does it matter? If we're all infected, aren't we just waiting to become one of them?"

Morgan rolled her eyes. Her tone became short and defensive. "What are you trying to say? Are you saying we're doomed? You're just ready to give up hope?"

AFTER LIFE

"I'm saying I don't know." Alex looked out the window, watching the bodies mindlessly bump into each other and then begin walking in a different direction. "I'm just wondering if the dead will ever stop rising. What if they just keep coming until there isn't anyone left to die?"

Morgan said nothing, not sure of what she was scared of more, the corpses outside, or the darkness that was creeping inside. She could see something changing in Alex's eyes. An emptiness that was ready to shatter him. She needed him to feel something. She wanted him to give in. She wanted him to make love to her and she wanted him to not feel guilty about it. Somehow, that would make it okay for her to not feel guilty.

His thumb started turning the dial again.

The dial passed 89.3 and a small disturbance in the static crackled in the speakers. The room, which was just filled with the murmur and laughter of the game players, fell silent immediately.

Alex slowly crept his finger backwards, turning the dial at the slowest pace he could. The static shuddered, fading out into a wobble of bass tones. The tones began to form words as he pushed his thumb against the dial, trying to push it only a millimeter more.

"Bravo-One, are you inbound on target? Over."

"Andrews, are you seriously going to talk like that?"

"This is Alpha-Base. Are you inbound on the target? Over."

"We're like, fifteen minutes away from the drop zone. Maybe less."

"Roger that. Fifteen minutes. Over."

The radio fell silent and Alex looked down at the group on the floor. All of them stared at him with their eyebrows lifted.

"Alex?" Morgan began, but he held his finger to his lips, leaning his ear closer to the speakers of the boom-box as he turned up the volume.

"Was that... it sounded like the army," Omar said, lifting himself into a more upright position.

"Shh!" Alex demanded, holding his hand out flat to silence the room.

The radio spoke again. "Bravo-One? This is Alpha Base, do you copy? Over."

"Yeah, what do you want Andrews? We're just pulling up now. I'll let you know."

"Bravo-One, do you have visual confirmation on the target? Over."

"It's sort of hard not too. Those fuckin things are everywhere."

"Is the Humvee holding up? Over."

"Yeah. Those things can't touch us, let alone keep up with us. They're movin slow as shit now."

"Bravo-One, can you place the bomb in the center of the crowd. Repeat, can you declare target on center of the enemy crowd. Over."

"Screw you, Andrews. It ain't gonna matter where we plant this thing."

Alex looked up at the group again, this time he held fear in his eyes. "They're going to bomb... they're going to bomb the zombies!"

"Where?" Morgan and Emma asked at the same time.

"I don't know!" Alex said. Then perking his head toward the apartment door, he yelled, "Frank! Get in here!"

Frank came running into the room, surprised to see no visible emergency.

"The radio." Alex tried to explain, "We can hear the Army on the radio. They're going to blow up the zombies!"

"What?" Frank asked, a look of concern cracking his face.

Alex shrugged his shoulders as the voice came back on the radio.

"Okay Andrews, we got it set up, send us the detonation codes."

"Roger that, Bravo-One. Stand by for detonation code. Over."

Alex looked at Frank, confused.

"Detonation code?" Frank looked horrified. "They only need codes to... oh shit."

"What is it?" Morgan yelled, seeing the look of fear strike across Frank's face.

"We need to get downstairs," Frank said without thinking. "Oh shit. We need to get... fuck where do we go?"

"What is going on?" Alex asked, standing up from his seat.

"They are going to be setting off a very big bomb. Somewhere close enough for us to hear their radio chatter," Frank's eyes looked deadly serious. "A very, very big bomb."

Alex's face went white. The military was still active, at least in some degree. But, instead of giving him hope, they had just become more dangerous than the corpses.

"Bravo-One, the code is as follows..."

"We need to move!" Frank yelled.

"Grab the guns," Alex yelled back. "We can... we can fight our way down the stairs. We can close the doors as we go! The stairwell!"

"Help me carry Omar!" Morgan yelled at Emma as they both knocked the board game from his lap.

Ethan came running into the hallway as Frank tossed him a pistol. Ethan held up his hands at the last second, awkwardly catching the gun.

"What's going on?" he asked, pointing the barrel of the pistol at the floor.

"We need to clear the stairs! Fast!" Frank yelled, lugging the shotgun toward the stairwell door.

Mr. Peterson stumbled out from his apartment, obviously waking up from a nap and looking confused, "Why are we doing that?"

"Don't ask questions, Dad!" Emma screamed. "Just follow us!"

Frank reached the stairwell door and waited until Alex and Ethan stood behind him, each holding a pistol. Alex still held the boom-box in his other hand.

Frank gripped the door handle and turned toward the group to say, "We need to move fast. We need to secure all the doors before they can flood the stairwell and group up on us. I'll fire until the shotgun is dry, then you two cover me with the pistols while I reload. Got it?"

Ethan and Alex gave him single, determined nod and lifted their guns into a ready position. Frank turned the knob on the door and pulled it open, thrusting the flashlight on the barrel of his shotgun into the darkened doorway.

A scream let out from a few steps down and a man began running up, his arms outstretched when he saw the group of fresh meat. Frank fired off a single round, blowing the decaying flesh of the man's head and left shoulder into tiny pieces. The corpse fell, tumbling down the stairs, only to be leapt over by a young woman running up the stairs.

Frank stepped through the doorway, meeting the woman halfway on the staircase. He waited until she was dangerously close before he pulled the trigger, nearly disintegrating her upper torso. Frank pointed the barrel down the staircase, spotting three more corpses running from a floor below. The group could hear the moans of many more below them. Frank began unleashing rounds from the shotgun, slamming the pump-action back and forth between shots. Corpses began dropping, but more continued running up the steps.

Just as they reached the door to the second floor, Frank let loose his last two rounds into the doorway before slamming shut the metal door that had been propped open by a janitor's broom.

"I'm dry!" he yelled, dropping to one knee to start loading more shells into the shotgun.

Ethan and Alex looked at each other before pointing their flashlights down the stairs and saw the horde of people clamoring up the steps toward them.

Alex began squeezing his trigger wildly, landing rounds in the first two zombies climbing the stairs. The corpses stumbled for a second when the rounds hit them in the chest. Ethan landed two rounds in one head and that zombie dropped to its knees. The corpses behind the first row shoved the unmoving corpse out of the way and rose past, joining the lead zombie in the climb. Alex raised the barrel a tiny bit and squeezed the trigger again, sending a bullet into the lead corpse's head.

Again the zombies behind just trampled over, like a wave of corpses rolling toward the beach. Alex and Ethan kept squeezing, barely able to hold the flood of bodies at a standstill.

Frank finally finished loading his shotgun and yelled, "Ready!" before standing up and unleashing a blast into the faces of the flood. Heads exploded, destroying two or three brains at a time.

Frank, with a look of grimacing persistence, began the group's slow advance. Cutting down the wall of corpses with blast after blast from his shotgun, Frank soon found himself covered in the gore of the splattering flesh. Bodies fell to the sides as the group pushed past, climbing over the corpses that had begun to pile up on the ground.

Again Frank took a knee, loading the last of his shotgun shells. Again, Ethan and Alex barely kept the flood of bodies at bay. Frank stood up again, this time taking slow aim, trying to maximize the blast of every shell. Just as they pushed toward the first floor doorway that led to the back parking lot, Frank's shotgun ran dry.

They stopped at a standstill, only a few feet away from the last metal doorway that they needed to close. Frank slung the shotgun over his shoulder and took a step back, letting Ethan and Alex step forward.

They tried to advance the few feet more they needed, but found themselves only able to drop one corpse at a time. They were barely able to match the speed of the mass of bodies pouring in from the parking lot.

Morgan shifted Omar's weight toward Emma and yelled, "Take him!"

For a moment, Emma thought fear had gotten the best of Morgan and that she was running away, but Morgan only ran a few steps up the stairwell. She stopped and leaned down toward a corpse dressed as a policeman. She dug into his belt and pulled out a revolver.

Running down past Omar and the Petersons, she joined Alex and Ethan, firing into the crowd that poured from the doorway.

Alex's heart sank when he saw the slide of his pistol drop back, revealing the empty chamber. Two shots later, Ethan's pistol did the same. Morgan pulled the trigger and heard the hammer on her pistol make a click noise.

Frank flashed an instantaneous look at the guns before leaping at the crowd of zombies. He screamed a guttural yell, throwing his arms out wide to grab onto both corpses that pushed through the door. Frank's boots dug into the ground and he tried to throw the power of his legs into shoving the group of corpses back through the doorway.

The corpses grabbed onto Frank, opening their mouths wide before their teeth sunk into his arms. Blood began dropping from the bites as they slowly chewed the meat they tore from him.

"Push me!" Frank yelled in a strained voice back at the group, who stood in a horrified stun.

Alex broke free from his stare and ran forward, shoving Frank's back. Ethan jumped down to join him. Soon Mr. Peterson and Morgan were behind them pushing as well.

Frank screamed in pain as the zombies kept biting at him. More and more blood fell from the gaping wounds. As the group finally managed to move the mass of zombies out the door who now feasted upon Frank, his head fell back, his face white with blood loss. After he gave Frank one last shove out the doorway, Alex grabbed the metal door and slammed it shut, gasping for breath when the lock latched.

"Frank!" Morgan screamed.

Fists pounded against the doorways on all the second and first floor, echoing in the brick stairwell.

The radio cut into the pounding. "Okay Andrews... we're outside the blast zone."

"Copy that. Bravo-Two is also ready for detonation. Over."

"Let's see some fireworks."

Everyone looked at each other, hoping someone else would tell them what to do. Their minds froze at the thought of Frank's death and the impending attack that was about to explode. Too much adrenalin coursed through their veins.

"Get down on the floor!" Alex yelled, having no advice to give. "Cover your heads!"

The group sat in the rumble of fists on metal, broken only by the radio squealing when no one spoke. Morgan and Alex sat next to each other, staring into each other's eyes. They held both hands, their fingers interlaced. They both squeezed so hard their hands screamed with pain. Yet, neither let go.

Emma whimpered, digging her face into her father's chest. Ethan prayed out loud, reciting what he could remember of the Lord's prayer. Omar leaned against the wall, his hands covering his head.

A high pitch squeal pierced the volume of the pounding and the static of the radio. Then the ground shook and a *POP* vibrated the very air around them. A low rumble followed that got louder as it rushed near them suddenly becoming deafening and crumbling the walls above them, throwing debris across the stairwell before dropping it down on their heads.

The ceiling began to fall down and the stairs themselves began to crumble. The steel bent under the impact and crumpled down toward the floor. Screams and yelps of pain cried out. Eventually the stairs began to create a shield over the group, forming a steel nest that barely held the massive pieces of wall inches away from their heads.

AFTER LIFE

Day 23

4:01 pm

Long minutes passed before the ringing in their ears stopped and the last rumble fell away with the dust. Morgan called out first, asking if everyone was alright.

The Petersons called back.

Ethan coughed and gave a weak, "My leg…" before coughing more.

Alex fumbled with the small flashlight on the barrel of his pistol, finally managing to turn it on and cast it around the small enclosure the cave-in had created. Everyone was covered in dirt. Scratches and small amounts of blood mixed with the filth of the falling debris.

Ethan held his leg, a piece of steel lying next to it. The jagged steel was pointed toward a bloody gouge out of Ethan's leg. Ethan held it tightly.

"It's okay. It looks worse than it is," Ethan said, moving his foot around to show he still had control of it.

Alex turned the flashlight toward Omar and saw the boy slumped over with a pile of rubble crushing his lower body. A large pool of blood covered the ground and he didn't move.

"Omar?" Emma whimpered, spitting out dirt as she spoke.

"Oh shit," Alex spoke. Above him debris fell when the weight of the rubble hanging above them shifted.

"Emma," Mr. Peterson began, but suddenly realized he had nothing to say. He had no words to offer his daughter. He simply held onto her, stopping her from going to the boy.

It didn't take long for Omar to start twitching, his mouth growling with hunger, but unable to move from under the fallen wall.

"Oh my god! I knew something was wrong with him. He was infected!" Mr. Peterson spit.

Alex screamed, unable to stay calm with everything that just happened. "Don't you fucking get it! We're all infected! We all change into those things if we die!"

The metal beams that used to support the staircase let out a wrenching squeal as they bent under the stress of the weight. Larger pieces of debris above them fell.

"We need to get out of here," Alex said, trying to lower his voice unsuccessfully.

Morgan wiped the dirt from her eyes. "Maybe the bomb killed them. Maybe there isn't anything out there. Maybe it's safe to go out."

"Maybe," Alex said quietly. The metal staircase above them suddenly bent, letting out another horrific sound and dropping more dirt on to all of them. "Either way, we can't stay here. Mr. Peterson, help me with the door."

Mr. Peterson crawled toward where Alex had turned on the flashlight again. He handed the gun to Morgan and she pointed it at the door. A beam from the staircase had fallen over the door, making it impossible to open the door inward.

AFTER LIFE

"Mr. Peterson, get on that end of the beam and help me lift it up. When we raise the beam Morgan, you open the door and get it under the beam so we can drop it and get out."

Everyone nodded silently at each other and the two men started to lift. Mr. Peterson and Alex grunted as they elevated the beam, causing hunks of dirt and debris to fall down again.

Just as the beam inched over the doorway, Alex grunted out, "Now!"

Morgan yanked the door, the metal screeching against the metal of the stairway beam. Mr. Peterson and Alex dropped the beam on top of the door. They all looked out to see a parking lot full of corpses lying on the ground.

The corpses were nothing more than blown apart pieces. Even the ones fairly intact had smaller holes blown through them, but most were just piles of arms and legs. Torsos and heads.

The cars that weren't torn apart were flipped over, cast aside like children's toys. Morgan's Volkswagen was nowhere to be seen.

A gray cloud of debris blew through the air, making it impossible to see past the parking lot, but the city was quiet. The moans had stopped.

The group began wandering out of the building, holding their shirts over their mouths and squinting their eyes. Ethan limped slowly on one leg.

The wind was unnatural, blowing the gray dust that now covered everything into their faces at an incredible speed.

Alex looked back at the apartment building that used to stand three stories, and now saw only one wall still standing. Bricks, broken pipes and smoldering wreckage lay in a pile next to the broken wall. Alex's home was now nothing more than a covered grave.

"Let's go," Ethan said, tugging on Alex's shirt. "I don't want to be outside longer than we have to be."

"One second," Alex said before stepping back into the building. Acting quickly, he found a large hunk of stone lying on the ground and stepped toward the writhing corpse of Omar. With a single smash, the stone splintered Omar's skull, flattening the brain inside. Omar's body stopped moving.

Alex tore the shirt off Omar's back before he walked back out into the whipping, gray wind, holding his hand to block the ash from going into his eyes. He began walking around the blown up corpses, looking closely at the pile. He stopped and started digging his hands into the gray body parts.

He stood up, holding the shotgun that was strapped to Franks back.

He snapped off the flashlight taped to the barrel of the empty gun and slung the weapon over his shoulder.

Checking to see if the flashlight still worked he stepped back to the group. He made no eye contact while he wrapped Omar's shirt around Ethan's leg, trying to stop the bleeding that looked bright red compared to the gray of everything else.

When he finished, the group stuck close to the crumbled wall of the building as they walked toward the street, trying to stay out of the howling wind and still afraid that the corpses littering the ground would rise up at any moment.

When they made it to the front of the building, Alex squinted even tighter, trying to peer down the city block. Rubble covered the sidewalks and street, crushing cars and corpses with indiscretion. Buildings that once towered into the sky lay in piles, broken shells of their former height. Smoke and fire poured out from nearly every building, and any loose part of rubble was tossed aside in the wind.

"My god," Alex said, his face now chalky white from the dust that covered his body. "What did they do?"

"There's nothing left," Morgan said, trying to catch her breath without inhaling all the particles in the air.

"We survived," Mr. Peterson grunted, spitting dust out of his mouth. "That's what matters. And now we know the military is still out there. They're still fighting! This is a good thing!"

"Those guys didn't really sound professional or... they just didn't sound like they knew what they were doing. And besides, even if it really was the army, I don't think it's a good sign that they've resorted to bombing American soil." Alex said this as he turned his back on Mr. Peterson, uninterested in any debate the man had to offer. "If they're ready to flatten a major city, it's obvious the ground war isn't going well."

"Was it nuclear?" Ethan asked, turning around to try and completely take in his surroundings. "Should we be out in the radiation?"

"We'd be dead if it was nuclear," Alex said. "It was just a really big bomb. Even so, we should find somewhere that's still standing. Somewhere safer."

The group stood, trying to decide a direction to move when a moan erupted down the street. They immediately started moving the opposite way. As they made their way down the block, all of them found pieces of wood to use in case they needed to defend themselves. Ethan held his more as a walking stick, while everyone else gripped theirs like a weapon, held out in front of them defensively.

Alex stopped at the corner of every building, looking into the alleyway for movement. The farther they moved, the more often they heard moans. When they reached a major intersection, they saw a group of corpses moving across the street. All of them had been blown apart pretty badly and hobbled on legs with barely any muscles left.

"Their bodies were pretty damaged," Alex said to the line of survivors that trailed behind him, all leaning against the building they hid at the corner of.

A fire raged across the street, consuming three of the four buildings, but slowly creeping toward the last. Alex knew further down the block, the area became spread out, filled with townhouses instead of apartment buildings.

"Come on," Alex said, stepping out from the corner. "If we run, they'll never be able to keep up."

"Alex," Morgan said, looking at Ethan.

Alex denied the fact that his mind's first thought was to leave Ethan. That he would only slow them down.

"Come here," Alex said, putting his arm around Ethan so he had something to brace himself on. "We're going to move fast so just hop on one leg and put your weight on me, okay?"

The group hesitantly stepped out with them and broke into a run when the zombies noticed them. All five of them ran down the street, leaving footprints in the ashy dirt, only to be blown away in the whipping wind.

Alex held his arm up to shield his eyes as he looked down the neighborhood street. The houses that once stood on the street were decimated, blown into piles of wood and nothing more. The cement foundations were all that showed him where the buildings once stood.

Alex wanted to stop and stare in horror at the devastation, but the creeping danger of the outside world pushed him forward. He kept running, his lungs inhaling the ash as he gasped for breath. He pushed his out of shape body past its limitations, continuing down street after street of rubble, lugging Ethan along with him.

Finally, Morgan grabbed his sleeve, gasping the words, "Alex... stop..."

The group slowed down behind him, standing in the middle of the neighborhood street. Mr. Peterson bent over, leaning on his knees while his body coughed out his exhaustion. Emma looked behind them, only seeing a few corpses dragging their feet in the distance. Ethan leaned against Alex, rubbing his wounded leg with a strained look on his face.

The farther away they ran, the thinner the ash was. Alex was definitely leading them away from the epicenter of the blast.

"We need…" Alex panted. "We need to keep moving."

"Just give us a second," Morgan said, looking Alex directly into his eyes, telling him to slow down without saying a word.

"Okay," Alex said. "Just keep your eyes open. If you see any corpses…"

Ethan stretched his back, scanning the cloud of ash, trying to see past the blowing debris. Across the street he saw someone dragging their body across the front yard. He said Alex's name and pointed at the torn apart body moving, ever so slowly, toward them.

Alex left Ethan balancing on one foot while he stomped across the street, and walked across the lawn to the body. Slamming his hunk of wood into the body's skull, he crushed the brain under the impact. He turned and walked back over to the group.

"Let's keep moving," he said. "We'll go slower, I promise."

The group groaned and stood up, moving down the road slowly. Alex was actually impressed with the constitution they were all showing and walked next to them, keeping his eyes on the distance, always looking for movement. They walked for blocks, seeing only more destruction in the gray fog of dirt that hovered over the city. The wind carried a hollowness that even a city of dead could not create.

Soon the street crept up a hill, the sides of which used to be lined with trees. Now only splintered stumps lay in the ground, torn from the rest of their growth. The houses here had a bit more left to the ground floor, but the walls still stood with gaping holes in them, offering the group no protection.

"We need to get out of the city, while we still can." Mr. Peterson growled his words, obviously making a demand more than offering a suggestion.

Alex hated to admit it. "You're right. We need to use this opportunity." He looked around at the sky, trying to make sense of his directions. "We can cut over to 35W and head north, travel on US 8 into Wisconsin. Totally bypass Hudson."

"You want to see your Father," Morgan said.

"He said he was safe. There's not a lot of people there. It's..." Alex looked at the ground. "It's the only idea I have."

"No, it's a good one," Morgan said.

Emma shook her head, unwilling to look into the eyes of any of her companions, "We lost all of our food. All of our things. All that work."

Mr. Peterson sounded annoyed, "It will be fine, Emma. We can find more food. We can start over. There's no reason to cry."

Alex scowled at the man, pushing his anger toward the insensitive father deeper down. He tried to empathize with Mr. Peterson. He knew the man was still in denial. Alex knew that Mr. Peterson still believed the world would go back to the way it was. Even with the destruction that blotted out the sky.

Alex continued walking east, down another neighborhood road, spotting a scattering of slow-moving corpses up ahead.

He gripped his bloody piece of wood in his hand, readying the make-shift weapon for even more violence.

AFTER LIFE

Day 23

7:02 pm

Minneapolis burned in the distance, a cloud of gray ash hovered within the skyline. The entire city looked as if it smoldered, emanating smoke in a massive plume, blocking out the sun itself. Far in the distance, in the other direction, a blackened blotch hovered in the sky where St. Paul once stood.

The group stood on a hilltop, looking out over what was left of the buildings below them. They stood in silence, none of them knowing words that fit the situation, much less their own emotions. Emma was the only one allowing herself to react. The only one allowing herself to feel.

She cried for Omar, the heart of youth unhindered by the short amount of time they spent together. She whimpered and even screamed a few times when she saw the state of the city. And, possibly more than anyone else, she still reacted to the dead.

Whether they had given up, assuming death was inevitable, or they simply had no emotion left to give, the rest of the group let out no screams, or showed anything like fear when faced with the few moving corpses left after the bomb.

They simply reacted with a blank look on their face as they smashed in the skulls of the bodies that still moved. With the color of the ash covering every square inch of the group, Emma could barely tell the difference between her companions and the walking dead.

Alex leaned over a barrier and looked at a road sign that hung on the highway below them. The sign hung sideways, dangling below the over pass.

US 8   15 MILES

He glanced across the highway and saw buildings that, besides broken windows and some missing shingles, looked fairly intact. He pointed them out to the group.

"Looks promising," Ethan said, noticing the same buildings Alex did.

"We should stop at the Wal-Mart," Mr. Peterson said, breathing heavy. "Once we get up north. Get supplies."

Alex cringed. He never thought he would have to set foot in his old job again, but he couldn't argue with Mr. Peterson's logic. Wal-Mart was gigantic and full of supplies they were going to desperately need. If it wasn't already looted. And it was close to the exit for US-8. Far enough away from the blast site to have survived.

Alex looked over the barrier at the highway below them, noticing that other than a randomly crashed car, the street was fairly clear.

"You're right," he agreed with Mr. Peterson. "We should stop there, but the trip will be a lot easier with a car. US 8 is still a long way down the road on foot. Ethan's leg just keeps bleeding with this much movement."

"We can search the homes," Morgan agreed. "It shouldn't be impossible to find someone's car keys."

"But-" Mr. Peterson started to argue, but the group was already walking across the overpass, toward the unhurt houses.

The streets were obviously victims of the initial outbreak of undead. Cars were crashed into telephone poles, trash was scattered across the street, doors hung open and windows were shattered, exposing the insides to the hungry corpses.

The group made their way down the sidewalk slowly and quietly, smashing the three corpses that shambled across the lawn as silently as possible. Alex realized then that the quiet planks of wood were better weapons than the loud guns would have been.

Who knows how many zombies would have been drawn out by gunfire?

The first two houses they passed had no car parked in the driveway, but the third garage was still closed. Alex ran up to the door and peeked inside the window, seeing a minivan parked inside. He held his thumb up in the air, silently motioning that his search was a success. The group hurried across the front yard, meeting Alex at the side door of the house. Alex pushed open the door, which was swinging freely in the breeze.

The sunlight that was barely breaking through the gray clouds above them had started to fade in the evening hours and when they stepped inside the house the darkness was endless in its blackness. The two beams from Alex and Morgan's flashlights clicked on, striking across the kitchen. The table was knocked over and a fish tank lay smashed on the floor.

"Blood!" Morgan pointed out, seeing a splatter of red on the corner of the counter top.

Alex handed the flashlight to Ethan and stepped toward the entryway to the living room, peaking down the hallway that lead back to bedrooms. The entire house looked like it had been ransacked, yet nothing looked missing.

When he looked into the living room, he saw a man lying on the carpet. He motioned for Morgan to move forward and she was instantly next to him. Her plank of wood was at the ready as she pointed her flashlight into the room.

Alex stepped into the room slowly, placing his foot gently down onto the carpet. He took two more precisely chosen steps, bringing him right next to the corpse. He held the piece of wood over him, ready to bring it crashing down on the body's head. He kicked, instinctively taking an immediate step away as soon as he had touched the corpse.

The body didn't move.

Alex glanced at Morgan and saw him shrug his shoulders. He kicked the body again, then leaned down and poked the head with the piece of wood, noticing a giant butcher knife stabbed into the top of the man's skull.

"I think he's dead. *Dead* dead," Alex said. He knelt down, setting the piece of wood on the floor next to the body. His hands started digging in the pockets of the pants, but found nothing more than a wadded up dollar bill and some change. Alex kept his eyes on the body and stood back up, joining Morgan who was beginning to move down the hallway.

"We'll search the cupboards," Ethan said to Alex as he passed through the kitchen. Alex nodded at him, a look of great seriousness shadowing his eyes.

Morgan stepped up to the first door, which was closed and still looked secure. She wiggled the knob back and forth, realizing it was locked.

They checked the two bedrooms, finding them empty of any bodies. Drawers were overturned and clothes scattered across the entire room. After digging for a long time, they found no keys.

"The locked door must be the bathroom." Morgan said, nodding her head toward the only door they hadn't opened.

"I guess we need to check it." Alex looked around the dark kitchen, counting the few cans of baked beans the group had found in the back of the cupboard. "The keys have to be somewhere."

When he and Morgan stood on either side of the doorway, Alex reluctantly slammed his shoulder into the bathroom door, trying to knock it down. Morgan held out her hand and stepped across the hall from the door. She leaned against the wall and lifted her foot, smashing her shoe into the door three times before the wood finally caved in, splintering around the doorknob.

A scream erupted from the bathroom and a skinny, older woman's body leapt from the door, smashing Morgan against the hallway wall. The corpse's mouth snapped closed, its teeth clicking together as Morgan managed to brace its head away from her own.

Alex swung the piece of wood in his hand, connecting with the corpse's head. Decaying flesh helped the head tear clean off from the body, slamming into the wall before hitting the hallway floor with a low *thump*.

Morgan allowed herself to breath as she let go of the woman's body, letting the bluish-black corpse crumple to the floor. Greenish pus filled sacs on the skin broke open, releasing a tiny, dusty cloud of greenish gas.

"Sick. What is happening to their bodies?" Emma asked, turning her face away from the smell with her nose scrunched up.

"Look!" Alex beamed, stepping over the body into the bathroom. The woman's purse sat next to the sink, some of its contents spilled across the counter. Morgan shined her flashlight on the pile of items as Alex began digging through them. He heard the familiar sound of keys jingling together.

"Got'em!" Alex called out, holding up a ring of keys in the light.

"Thank God," Mr. Peterson said. "Now let's get out of here!"

Emma grabbed a grocery bag and filled it with the cans they had found. The group hurried out the door, scanning the driveway and street, half expecting it to be full of walking corpses again, but the dead had not returned.

Alex fumbled with the keys, trying three different ones before unlocking the garage door. The mini-van's key was easier to find, covered in molded plastic that made it feel bigger than the others. With a quick turn, the driver's side door opened and Alex slapped the button for the power locks.

"Everyone, get in," Alex yelled as he jumped into the seat and pushed the box on the sun visor, starting the slow crawl of the automatic garage door. The van started up and Alex pulled the shift lever into reverse before everyone was even seated. "Everyone ready?" Alex looked into the rear-view mirror, watching everyone settle into their seats.

Ethan slammed the side door shut and said, "Yeah, let's go."

The van pulled out into the street and Alex maneuvered it around two cars smashed into each other. He pushed harder on the gas when they reached the 35W exit, seeing a wider open road in front of them.

A whimper rumbled in the van as everyone's minds were given a moment to relax and catch up. The whimper came from Emma. The rest of the group felt nothing, their minds unable to grasp the severity of tragedy their lives had become.

AFTER LIFE

Day 24

12:56 am

Even though the moon was nearly full, the world around them still felt endlessly black. With only the headlights of the van lighting his way, Alex was driving very slow. Objects appeared suddenly in front of them, debris randomly scattered around the highway. He swerved around all three lanes, sometimes driving off the road to get around large pile-ups and an overturned semi-truck.

Bodies wandered amongst the cars occasionally, but moved slowly, easily outrun in the minivan. The destruction caused by the bombs became less apparent the farther north they drove. The destruction of the dead was still overwhelming.

Alex hated to admit it, but the gray cloud that covered Minneapolis had made the world feel cleaner in some way. The monotone gray that became the color of everything was somehow preferable to the honest colors that they were re-entering. The colors of death, trash, and the occasional dried pool of blood

The world looked so shattered that Alex expected to find a giant crack somewhere on the earth, opening wider with every passing second. His mind felt as if it were seizing when he tried to comprehend how mankind was capable of such mindless devastation in such a short period of time. Being outside the security of the apartment was truly forcing Alex to face the reality of the world. A world he had been seeing from afar. A world that was always "over there". Safely in the distance.

Now the world surrounded him, strangling him with its endless vacancy. The hopelessness he felt truly scared him in its severity. The creeping approach of death hovered behind his shoulders, sending a breathy chill down his spine. He looked to Morgan, fearful she would sense his panic. A surge flooded to his lips when he imagined having to tell her they had no hope. He thought about how he would tell her he failed. How he would tell her they were going to die.

His lips let loose a single sob and he realized tears were already running down his face. He wiped his eyes, focusing his vision on the road again. His grip on the steering wheel tightened, and he flushed the moment of emotion from his body with a deep breath. His body felt securely empty again.

"Do you want to go to your house?" Alex asked in a monotone voice. "We have enough gas. If you want. See if there's anything left? I mean-"

"No," Morgan cut him off. "I don't care about that stuff. I don't need anything from... from..."

She let her mind think about her possessions for an instant. Her house. Her things. She let herself mourn their loss for a brief shadow of a second before knowing, once again, that those things were meaningless now. She stared past her reflection in the window, unable to look at her own image any longer. Covered in thick, white ash and only colored by bloody scrapes, she looked like she was already dead and just hadn't accepted it. She wondered if this was how the corpses outside felt.

Past her image was a world that looked like she felt. Torn apart and damaged, it was as if someone had suddenly shaken the whole earth. She watched the view outside her window change from the white ash of Minneapolis, to the slightly more intact suburbs. The buildings still stood here, but so did the dead.

Alex began swerving the van even more, sometimes knocking into the corpses with a, "Well? Get out of the damn way!" exploding from his lips.

Morgan's hope that the military had taken care of most of the zombies was lost. Seeing that the suburbs looked just as infected as Minneapolis lessened the chances that anywhere was safe.

She knew she couldn't go much further. She knew she wasn't going to be able to run for the rest of her life. She needed to get back inside. Her anxiety propelled the van down the road by itself.

When she glanced at Alex and saw a single tear roll down his face, she felt guilty. She knew in her mind that he needed her. He needed her to comfort him. She knew she should reach out. Touch him. Her head turned, looking back out the window, her mind no longer feeling. Not even guilt.

Ethan sat in the back seat of the minivan. His eyes had glazed over, his brain not even functioning enough to comprehend the images that washed past his window. He stared at a smudge on the glass, thinking about absolutely nothing. He simply stared, letting his thoughts be still. He felt his mind was unwilling to struggle any longer.

Mr. Peterson wanted to comfort his daughter, but he knew better. He knew she had to toughen up and she had to do it fast. He knew she was too weak and if anything happened to him, he didn't want to leave behind a victim.

He had been hard on her because he knew the world would do the same. He didn't want to raise someone who expected the world to treat her with respect and love and give her hugs and kisses. Mr. Peterson knew better. He glared at the outside world, his body tense with anger.

Emma tried to lean against him, but his body felt like stone, unmoving in its solidity. She cried to herself, finding herself scared of not only the world they found outside, but the people she was traveling with. She felt as if she was the only person left that hadn't changed into an unfeeling monster. She thought of Omar and wondered if he would have changed too.

If he had the chance, would he have given up on life like everyone else?

Alex began slowing down at gas stations and convenience stores, hoping to find something intact and full of supplies. Nothing they passed was worth the risk of getting out of the minivan. Gas pumps lay on the ground, dry. Windows were smashed and the shelves inside had been looted weeks ago.

He knew that outside, they would no longer be gatherers. Now, they would be scavengers.

The exit sign for Forest Lake appeared in the headlights and Alex gradually moved the minivan into the exit lane, dodging a man and woman standing in the road, neither of whom had arms. Only stringy pieces of flesh hung from their torso.

Police cars were at the bottom of the exit ramp, barely blocking the road. Alex surmised that it was a barricade at one point, but had been broken through long ago. He nudged the minivan between the two cars, scraping the side of the van against the bumper of a squad car and then pressed on the gas, hanging a right toward Wal-Mart.

His old job.

He got the same sinking feeling when he saw the sign hovering over the parking lot as he did when he saw it on his way to work. The creeping feeling that the next eight hours of his life belonged to someone else. The feeling that he needed to become someone else while he was there in order to keep his job.

Now he needed to become someone else in order to survive.

It did not take long for the street to become thicker with walking corpses. Alex kept the minivan at a speed fast enough to knock down any body that got in his way, but stayed as slow as possible, still relying on the headlights to reveal any cars, or debris that littered the road.

As the parking lot came into view, Alex shuddered at the number of zombies that had gathered outside the giant store.

"Oh my god." Morgan gasped, pushing herself back in her seat away from the windshield.

"I'm turning around, this isn't worth it," Alex said as he began to yank on the wheel, curving the minivan across the street, knocking over a group of the undead bodies.

"No! Wait!" Mr. Peterson yelled. "Look at the doors!"

The group stared out the window, trying to peer through the horde of zombies blocking the view of the front doors. There, across the sea of bodies, they saw two sets of glowing doors in the darkness.

"There must be people!" Ethan yelled out. "They have power!"

Alex continued the minivan turning and made a 360 degree turn, speeding up as they came out of it. The minivan's engine whined as he floored the gas pedal, aiming the nose directly at the front doors. Bodies began hitting the van hard, getting knocked back into the bodies standing next to them. Soon corpses began clinging to the sides of the van, dragging behind the speeding vehicle. The bodies became so thick near the entrance, the tires began bouncing over corpses laying on the ground, throwing everyone inside around in their seats. As the minivan slammed into a group of four corpses, Alex slammed on the breaks, seeing the glowing doors twenty feet in front of him. Alex squinted his eyes, trying to peer inside the doors.

"If we're getting out, we need to go now!" Ethan yelled, watching the massive group of corpses that filled the parking shamble toward the minivan.

Alex and Morgan leapt out the front doors of the minivan as the rest of the group filed out of the side door. Alex left the minivan running and dashed toward the front doors of the superstore.

Morgan helped Ethan while the Peterson's were right behind Alex. The glass of the automatic doors was smashed open, allowing the group to slide through the frames of the doors one at a time.

Once inside, the group stopped, staring up at a wall of shelving units that towered in front of them. The wall was nearly twenty feet in the air and completely blocked off the second set of doors. Bright lights shone from above the shelves, lighting up the entire entryway.

Everyone smashed up against the wall and began screaming over the shelves, turning around periodically to watch the advancing mob outside.

"Help!" Emma screamed.

"We're alive! Let us in!" Mr. Peterson shouted in a hollow voice.

Alex turned around and saw the corpses walking across the parking lot reach the minivan. He knew there was no turning back now.

"Everyone climb!" Alex yelled, grabbing a shelf high above him and lifting himself up. Mr. Peterson was the next to leap to action, grabbing onto shelves and starting his ascension next to Alex.

As Alex reached the top, he saw the zombies reach the front of the store and start filing through the doors, the broken glass tearing their flesh. When he looked down, he saw the group struggling to get up the wall of shelves fast enough.

Mr. Peterson had already lifted himself to the top, panic fueling the overweight man's sudden climb. Emma was near him, but Ethan and Morgan were still quite low. Morgan was trying to help the nearly one legged Ethan up every step.

"You've got to hurry!" Alex yelled, still at the top. Mr. Peterson and Emma began climbing down the other side.

Ethan began to speed up, but Morgan was struggling underneath him, still near the bottom of the wall. Alex could see her legs were still within grasp of the corpses that had almost reached her.

He looked down, his heart pounding in his ears when his mind realized that Morgan was going to die. His body began to shake and his fingers quivered convulsively as he tried to do something... *anything* to save her.

Ethan's hand reached up, his hand open, waiting for Alex to help him over the top. Alex grasped onto his arm and looked him deep in the eyes.

"I'm so sorry," he said quietly, before he released his grip, letting Ethan fall backwards.

Morgan screamed as Ethan fell past her. His face was in silent shock as he landed on the group of zombies that were just reaching for Morgan's legs. All the zombies that had filled the entrance to the store lost interest in Morgan and focused on Ethan, their arms reaching for his flesh. His body was torn apart in a hundred directions by the grasping fingers of the undead mob. His screams of pain were inhuman.

Alex helped a whimpering Morgan to the top of the wall, her arms still shaking with fear. His body was cold and sweaty, and his stomach felt like it was full of acid. His eyes became dry and itchy.

I just killed someone.

"Alex!" Mr. Peterson yelled from below.

Alex looked over the side of the shelving he sat on the top of. Down below, standing at the base of the wall and looking into the interior set of doors, Mr. Peterson stood with his hands in the air.

"They want you to get off their wall."

AFTER LIFE

Day 24

2:43 am

A tall, wide shouldered man with a thick black beard held Mr. Peterson at knife point. The knife was gigantic, more for display and intimidation than for any utilitarian purpose. A much skinnier man was holding Emma's arms behind her back. He looked the same age as the large man, but unhealthy. His skin was speckled red with blotches of white. He snarled, and when his lip lifted, it revealed only the only two teeth left in his mouth. Both men wore brand new clothes.

Two floodlights sat on either side of the door, the boxes they used to be packed in still sat next to them. Both lights were plugged into battery powered generators and were pointed outwards, but shone bright enough to light up the entryway.

Alex's mind tried to work fast, to figure out how to talk the group out of this situation, but all he could think about was Ethan. Alex saw his face and the look of shock as he fell to his death.

Guilt was hovering over him, waiting for him to relax and allow his mind to dwell so that it could strike. He knew if he allowed those thoughts to enter he would be crushed by the weight of it all, and so his mind refused to relax. It flooded his thoughts with memories of Morgan and how he had done it to save her. He was the hero.

Behind the two men covering the Petersons was a man a few years older than Alex. His skin was dark, with black hair trimmed short, and large sideburns that covered his very rounded cheeks. His eyes looked friendly behind square glasses, in sharp contrast to his bare arms covered in tattoos and the large fire axe he held in his hand.

"Are there any more of you?" the bearded man asked, as Morgan climbed down.

"No," Alex answered. "The rest... It's just us."

"Where are you from?"

"We came-" Morgan started, but found herself gasping.

"We came from Minneapolis," Alex finished for her. "We were heading toward Wisconsin. We just stopped here to... to look for supplies."

The man's eyebrows curved, as if he was pondering what Alex had told him.

"My name is Alex, this is Morgan, and those are the Petersons, Mike and Emma."

Emma struggled with the skinny man that held her, finally shouting, "Let me go!"

The bearded man nodded at the skinny man and Emma was released, allowing her to run to her father.

"I'm Harold," the bearded man said, his eyes never showing anger. "The man with the axe is Nathan and the one who was nice enough to unhand the girl is Jesse. Now that we're nice and acquainted, how about you hand over your shotgun?"

Alex shrugged and slung the gun off his shoulder, then tossed it to the bearded man saying, "Take it. I don't have shells for it anyway."

Harold caught the gun in one flabby arm and nodded. "Thanks."

"We didn't come here to start any trouble," Alex said. "We saw your lights and we didn't even know anyone else was alive."

Harold slung the shotgun over one shoulder and slid his knife into a leather sheath on his belt. His fingers scratched his hairy chin before he spoke. "Jesse and I will go tell Owen what we found. Nathan, put these guys in the break-room until we figure out what to do."

Jesse and Harold walked into the darkness, but Alex could see a glow coming from the back of the store, near where the electronics department was.

They walked through the grocery section, with only Nathan's flashlight to light their way. The shelves were ransacked, with boxes, cans, and packages of food scattered across the floor. Trash littered the aisles, and the smell of rotten vegetables and fruit was putrid in the air.

"Who is Owen?" Mr. Peterson asked, while Nathan began leading them toward the back of the store.

"Owen is…" Nathan hesitated. "He's in charge."

"In charge?" Alex asked, surprised at the explanation.

"I met him when the outbreak first happened," Nathan began to explain. "I knew something big was happening and I wanted to beat the rush for food and whatever else I would need."

Nathan pushed the swinging doors open that blocked off the back area of the store. A skinny hallway, lined with employee lockers, led deeper into the back rooms and eventually to the break-room. Alex remembered it all well, but now the back area felt oddly empty. What was normally filled with carts, returned or defective items, and employees scampering around on their breaks, was now stagnant and still. Like nothing had been touched in weeks.

"By the time I got here," Nathan continued, "I was far from the only one looking for supplies. This place was a mad house. People were running through the aisles, knocking each other over, yanking things out of each other's carts. The employees were trying their best, but…"

When they reached the break-room, Nathan held the door open and shined the flashlight into the room. The group shuffled into the doorway and Alex tried to push away the feeling he was being put into a prisoner's cell.

"From what people have said, someone was trampled near the camping stuff" Nathan was visibly struggling through his story, unhappy to relive the events. "Somebody actually dying made everyone stop. People were shocked back into reality when they realized the consequences of their actions. They actually slowed down and started to help each other." Nathan took a deep breath, fighting past his inner barriers so that he could move on with his story. "It didn't take long for the woman who died to get back up. She started biting the employees who were trying to cover up her body with a blanket. In the chaos that followed, the infection spread fast. People just ran, grabbing what they had in their carts and running for the doors. The violence followed them."

Everyone in the group had taken a seat at the tables in the break-room. Morgan scanned the vending machines, but saw only empty rings behind the broken glass. The soda machines were opened, showing their empty shelves inside. Nathan stood by the door holding the only light, but didn't give the appearance he was standing guard. His stance held no aggression, or defiance. He truly seemed to be opening up.

"Once the infected were outside, it was Owen that figured out how to lock the doors. At first we thought we were just going to be waiting for the police." Nathan shrugged and his head dropped. "Obviously we were wrong. Over the days, it was Owen that brought everyone together. It was Owen that really showed these people... he showed them that they didn't need to give up. They didn't need to change who they were to survive. He reminded us all that we're still human."

Alex wanted to discuss the topic, but his mind felt useless, still occupied with visions of Ethan's face as he was torn apart. Alex held his stomach as it began to churn, sending cold shivers down his back. His nerves were twisting his insides, punishing him for his resistance to the guilt.

"How many people live here?" Morgan asked.

Nathan cleared his throat before he answered. "There's twelve of us now." He cleared his throat again. "Those that didn't run outside and die in the parking lot, died while we tried to build a barrier for the doors. We tried stacking up the shopping carts first, but it was a dumb, knee jerk idea. The carts were weak and those things started knocking the wall over within a few days. By the time we got the shelves moved in from the grocery department..."

"I'm sorry," Morgan weakly offered him.

"It's okay. I didn't even know those people. I know that sounds horrible, but so many people have died that..." Nathan shrugged, casting off his inner contemplation. "My old lady is the one I'm worried about. She was pregnant with my-" Nathan stopped mid-sentence to lift his glasses and wipe his eyes with an open palm. "I'm sorry. I don't know why I'm telling you this. I just get lost in my thoughts sometimes."

Alex held up his hand. "It's okay. I think we're all a bit lost."

The group sat in silence in the near dark for a few long minutes, eyes darting around the room, taking in their surroundings. Alex had been in the room many times before and could not help but get lost in the decorations covering the walls. Photos for a "cutest baby picture contest," results for the money collected on "jeans day," and reminders of the company motto filled the walls with bright colors that were muted in the darkness.

Alex found himself deep in the daydreams of how simple his past used to be when the door opened and an aged man walked in. The man's frame had a thin height and the light from Nathan's flashlight accentuated the man's white hair. His eyebrows were curly and random, casting white wisps of hair in every direction. A permanent scowl etched onto his thin skinned forehead was barely masked by the man's smile.

He held out his hands in a warm acceptance and introduced himself. "Hello! My name is Owen."

The group mumbled their introductions weakly, fighting past their own exhaustion. Owen nodded as each person said their name and quietly repeated the name to himself.

"And where are you traveling from?" Owen asked, crossing his arms across his tight flannel.

"Minneapolis," Mr. Peterson answered, showing a certain annoyance with the upbeat attitude of the old man.

"Really!" Owen sounded excited. "How on earth did you get out?"

"Yesterday." Alex let himself speak, pushing aside his thoughts. "The military, or someone set off a bomb in the middle of the city. Our building was caught in the blast, but we managed to survive. When we went outside, there were only a few corpses left standing."

"Oh, that is just wonderful!" Owen said, his voice sounding overly dramatic and grandfatherly. "The military! We hadn't heard anything on the radio. We tried to keep our hopes up." Owen glanced at Nathan who gave him a forced smile and a nod of agreement.

"I'm still not convinced we're winning, or that we should expect rescue anytime soon," Alex said, his voice sounded like sandpaper. "The guys on the radio, they made it sound like this was a last ditch effort."

"Well," Owen smiled, clapping his hands together. "That's just fine. As long as it worked."

"I didn't say it did," Alex said, his voice coming from the darkness. "Those bombs made a mess of things, but there are plenty of bodies still walking around out there."

"What do you mean? You were able to escape."

"As soon we got a few miles from my building the roads were covered in them."

Owen's smile slowly fell from his face. He looked to the floor, gathering his thoughts before he spoke. "Perhaps once they clear out the highest concentration they can move in and clear out the few remaining."

"The few?" Alex's voice was beginning to strain, anger boiled through his lips.

Morgan finally stood up from her chair and spoke loudly, nearly yelling her question. "Have you looked outside lately? Your parking lot is full of those things."

Owen shook his head, still smiling. "No, I haven't been near the doors recently. There's really no reason to. We have everything we could possibly need right here. Now listen, most of the people are still asleep, so I'm gonna ask you to stay in here until they wake up and then we can make some proper introductions. No sense scaring anyone."

The group made no sounds of agreement, but neither did they make any noise of debate.

"Fine," Owen said, walking out the door. "We'll see you in a few hours."

Nathan left the flashlight behind and followed Owen, leaving the group in utter silence. No one talked, or dared speak their thoughts, too lost in a flood of emotional drain to make any sense. They simply curled up on the tables, resting their heads on packages of napkins Alex found in a cupboard.

They lay in safety and silence, yet no one slept.

Day 24

7:05 am

Morning came slowly, the silent hours of the night creeping by. Without windows, it was Nathan that alerted the group to the sunrise.

"Mornin everyone." His voice came from the doorway, shining a flashlight into the room. "If you want to follow me, I can take you to the bathroom."

The group crisscrossed through the clothing departments, noticing the rows of empty racks. It looked like the survivors had picked most of the shelves clean. In the distance Alex saw the same glow of lights from the back of the store near the electronics. He swore he heard music too.

As they got to the front of the store and passed the kitchen appliances, the aisles looked a little neater. The goods kept there were unneeded by looters or the men and women living in the store.

The pharmacy however, was nearly empty.

The group finally came to the western side of the store and walked into the seasonal department. During the right time of year a person could find holiday ornaments, Halloween costumes, or back-to-school supplies on the shelves. In the beginning of summer, the area was stocked with gas grills, lawn furniture, and gardening supplies.

"Head up to the front. Toward the daylight. One at a time," Nathan said, smiling. "There's a small outdoor area that's fenced off. It was used to store the shade plants, but it has a sewer drain you can-" Nathan shrugged, assuming he didn't have to explain any further.

Morgan held out her arms, ushering Emma to go first. The young girl didn't make eye contact, but just shook her head, holding her hands close to her chest.

"I'll go with you, okay?" Morgan said, holding out her hand.

Emma hesitated before she eventually grasped Morgan's hand slowly and the two of them walked toward the daylight coming from the front entrance to the department. A large metal shelving unit had been placed in front of the doors, but large windows surrounded the roof, letting in plenty of light. In the corner of the department was a large, metal wall that had been raised up to reveal a small outdoor enclosure.

The area had only a few shelves in it, lined with dead plants. Two of the walls were made of a chain link fence with a green tarp lining the inside. The roof was open to the air. The cement floor was stained with wetness around a large sewer drain in the middle of the room. A plastic lawn chair with a hole cut in the middle sat over the top. Outside in the early morning air, the moans of the dead could be heard from the parking lot.

"Oh gross," Emma said, covering her nose even though it didn't actually stink.

"I would tend to agree," Morgan said, stepping toward the makeshift toilet.

Once the group had all taken their turn, Nathan led them back toward the electronics department. As they walked past the toy department, Alex shook his head in disgust. He worked in that section of the store and used to be obsessed with collecting the tiny plastic action figures that now hung unused and useless on their pegs. Yet another shadow of his former life that mocked him.

The sound of country music came from behind shelves that had been moved to encircle an area normally full of CDs, DVDs and video games. In the circle of shelves, office chairs and a few short couches were arranged in small groupings. Most of them surrounded one large table that a group of people were eating breakfast on.

Three children sat on the floor near a pile of toys, eating dry cereal from the box. A woman helped one of the boys change out of his shirt and into a clean one. She stopped moving completely and simply stared when Nathan walked into the circle with the group.

"Hey everyone, can I have your attention?" Nathan said, smiling big as he held out his arms to present the group.

"Yes, yes, everyone quiet down, I have some people I want you to meet," Owen said, suddenly cutting in and standing up from his place at the breakfast table. He walked over to the group with the same grandfatherly smile he had the night before.

Placing his hand on Mr. Peterson's shoulder, he began the introductions, remembering every one of their names without any help. He introduced the Petersons as father and daughter and Morgan as Alex's girlfriend. Morgan smirked at Alex.

As each of their names were said aloud, the group of Wal-Mart survivors nodded their heads and mumbled hellos, obviously apprehensive of the newcomers.

"Now, for us." Owen said, taking a few steps closer to the table.

AFTER LIFE

"This is Brenda Barker," Owen placed his hands on a middle aged woman's shoulders. Her brown curly hair was cut short, and the woman wore far too much make-up, which looked even more out of place in the world now. Her smile was slight and awkward, looking like she was using all her strength to force the curl in her lip.

"She was..." Owen cleared his throat. "She *is* a teacher here in Forest Lake. She teaches science." He smiled as he moved down the row to the woman sitting next to Brenda.

"This is Rhonda." Owen squeezed her shoulders as he said her name, making her look up at him and smile. "She's in charge of our food supply, so if you get hungry you'll have to let her know." Alex recognized the bleached blond woman with leathery brown skin as an employee. She was quite a few years older than him and she worked in a different department, so he only knew her in passing. He watched her eyes as she made no reaction of acknowledgement, so he said nothing, assuming she didn't recognize him.

"This is Herman Leblanc." Owen motioned toward a middle-aged man with a receding blond hair line and glasses. The man wiped his mouth with a napkin and held up his hand to wave. "He was traveling down from Canada to a seminar in Minneapolis." Herman, still chewing his food, nodded at Owen's explanation.

Owen set his hand on the shoulder of the youngest girl at the table, which made her visibly uncomfortable. She was in her late teens and had jet-black hair, cut sharply so the front hung longer than the back. Her lip was pierced with a ring and her nose glittered with a small diamond. Her eyes looked huge in the light, but her head hung low, nodding as Owen introduced her.

"This is Ashley." Owen smiled big, a sort of titter in his voice. "We're not sure what she does." The rest of the group chuckled and Ashley rolled her eyes. "Ha, ha. I'm joking of course." As Owen walked over to the next man, Alex caught Ashley flashing Owen her middle finger, than nonchalantly running her hand though her hair.

"And this is Gary Harrison," Owen said, presenting a strong looking man in his late forties. A thick head of hair was combed neatly to the side and a gray t-shirt spread tightly across his thick barrel chest.

"Nice to meet you folks," Gary said, his hardened face breaking to smile.

"You already met Harold and Jesse," Owen said, then pointed to the three children playing on the floor. "And those are the kids: David, Tyler and Isabella." No explanation was given as to who their parents might be, which left the group to assume they were orphans.

"Wow." Morgan smiled, waving her hand at the elbow once. "I don't know if I'll remember all that right away so I'm apologizing now."

"Oh that's fine, dear," Brenda the science teacher said. "I get used to learning new names *and* forgetting them, every year that I have new students."

The group around the table laughed.

"You guys must be hungry," Rhonda said, standing up from her seat and walking toward a plastic storage bin.

"Actually I could really use something to drink," Morgan explained, smacking her tongue to illustrate the dryness.

"Of course!" Owen shouted in a cheery voice, "Anything you need, just let Rhonda know!"

Alex sat next to Morgan at the table and they both began slurping down the bottles of water set in front of them. Both looked at each other for an instant, both about to allow themselves to smile, but both quickly turning away and settling into their unemotional states.

"So, you guys are from Minneapolis?" Brenda the school teacher asked, finishing up the last bite of meat on her plate and wiping the crumbs from her mouth. When she set down the napkin, the white cloth was smeared with the red of her lipstick.

"Yeah," Alex answered at the same time as Morgan, but it was Alex that continued. "We were living in an apartment building there when the bomb went off."

"Bomb?" The large man named Gary asked, his fork freezing in the air as he raised it to his mouth.

"Uh, yeah."

"Yes!" Owen spit out, cutting off any explanation Alex could give. "Our new friends have seen proof that the military is still out there fighting!"

The group around the table began to murmur to each other. Most of them appeared excited by the news, but a few looked skeptical. Alex began to notice a glassy look in all their eyes. They looked exhausted.

"They blew up Minneapolis?" Gary asked, setting down his fork and frowning tightly at Owen.

"A final blow to the most infected area, most likely!" Owen assured the group.

"Was it that bad in the city?" Herman the Canadian businessman asked Alex, looking to Mr. Peterson after he spoke as if to acknowledge any input he might have as well.

Alex shrugged, looking to Owen to see if he would offer another answer for them.

"The streets were thick with those infected people," Mr. Peterson said. "It was like the whole goddamn city was outside our window. I doubt anyone there is still alive."

A few of the people gasped and Rhonda peeked at the children, looking to see if they had overheard the man's grim description. The children carried on as if nothing had happened.

"They blew up everything?" Herman asked. He spoke clearly and enunciated his words very deliberately.

"I think it was just one bomb," Alex answered. "But it was big."

"Did it work?" Jesse asked, whistling through his missing teeth.

Alex shrugged again. "Depends on what you mean by 'worked.'"

"Well, it got you out of the city." Owen smiled. "We can be thankful for that."

"I can't believe it." Rhonda looked teary-eyed as she plugged a hotplate into a battery powered generator and began to open a can of canned meat. "The military. I already feel safer."

"Leave it to our troops to save the world." Owen smiled, clapping his hands together. "Now, if everyone wants to settle in front of the big screen, we can start a movie soon."

Alex noticed that he felt fairly safe. He couldn't hear the moans of the dead all the way in the back of the store. Familiar noises like music and the movie starting lulled him into a childlike stupor. A place where he didn't need to feel guilty, or paranoid. A place where he didn't need to change into a murderer just to survive.

Morgan felt something was off. Something didn't feel right about the store. After being outside and seeing what was really happening, she just couldn't accept this way of life anymore. It felt like a dream.

But soon, even she began to get caught up in the feeling that everyone else shared. Any thoughts of fear, or apprehension washed away as she sipped her cup of coffee and then overheard Brenda and Herman talking about a cigarette break.

AFTER LIFE

Day 33

1:41 pm

As the days stretched on, Alex teetered between feeling comfortable and knowing something was wrong. When he saw Emma and Ashley trying on clothes and laughing, or saw the look on Morgan's face when she saw the stockpile of cigarette cartons, he knew they were in a good place. Some place they could make a life that wasn't a constant struggle. Some place safe. Some place that felt familiar.

When he saw Owen's defiance toward any change, or his insistence on making every decision – from what the group will eat for dinner to who's turn it is to clean – Alex became uncomfortable. He found the old man insincere and unsettling.

Owen acted nice enough, but his attitude changed depending on who he was talking to. In front of the group, he was always upbeat, steering every conversation into a positive area. With the men he showed his gentle, grandfatherly side, always speaking calmly. With the young women he acted more like a concerned father, asking questions constantly and simply listening without much verbal reaction. With the older women he spoke in a whimsical tone, cracking jokes and touching them when he laughed.

Alex couldn't take his eyes off the man, fascinated by what appeared to be a very conscious manipulation of the group. He also soon realized that Owen didn't actually "do" anything, never helping to clean, or cook. He was always sending others to run his errands for him. The group leapt at the chance every time they were asked. They were truly obedient.

That afternoon it was Gary's turn to choose music for the radio and a CD of Tom Petty's greatest hits echoed in the electronics department. Alex sat near the kids, allowing himself to be distracted from Owen's actions only by the innocence the children played with. The two boys moved around some Japanese action figures, while the girl colored in a coloring book with Snow White on the page. All of them were genuinely content, truly unaware of the events in the world.

He was jealous of them all.

Morgan gently touched the top of his head as she walked behind him, toward the pharmacy. The health and beauty section of the store was near the front, but still far enough away from the doors to be completely engulfed by darkness. Morgan dug through the boxes on the floor, finding everything but what she looked for. The pharmacy had been completely ransacked and hoping to find anything was an impossible wish.

Her flashlight scanned across the floor, falling on box after box of tampons, adult diapers, condoms, and vitamins. Most lay unopened, tossed aside like they were simply in the way.

AFTER LIFE

As she walked through aisle after aisle of medicinal goods, another flashlight beamed from the paint department. It floundered around in the air for a moment, than turned off.

Morgan watched the area in the darkness for a moment, than went back to her search. She kept digging through the boxes until she heard someone curse from the direction of the light. The flashlight in the paint department flickered again and then went out.

Morgan gave up her search and walked down the main wide aisle of the store, toward the back. When she reached the paint department she aimed her flashlight down the aisle she had seen the flicker of light come from. There, crouched on the floor was Rhonda, the woman who was in charge of food. Morgan had been uncomfortable around Rhonda ever since she had to place her first "order". The woman exposed her power over the group as if she were underappreciated and desperate for attention. She took every opportunity to mention the work she did, but ignored any attempts to help her.

"Rhonda?" Morgan said the name softly, letting her light fill the aisle.

"What?" Rhonda spun around as if she had been caught doing something. "Oh. Um... Morgan. Right?"

"Right."

"Oh, thank you. My flashlight went out."

"Oh." Morgan stepped forward, offering her the flashlight. "I was just over there." She pointed vaguely toward the pharmacy. "What are you doing?"

"Oh. Owen and I were talking. He thought maybe we should do some decorating. Help everyone brighten up their little rooms."

The group had sectioned off parts of the store into sleeping areas. Each person had their own bed that was usually surrounded by a series of poles with sheets hanging from them to create walls. Brenda, the school teacher, had become a sort of step-mom to the children and they all shared a large room. Other than them, everyone else slept alone.

Morgan had been happy when Alex setup his bedroom next to hers.

"Oh. That sounds nice." Morgan tried to sound genuine, but in reality she thought the idea felt foolish. She had a creeping feeling the entire store was infected with denial. "Do you need help?"

"Sure," Rhonda said. The attitude in her voice sounded forced. "You can hold the flashlight for me."

Morgan did so as the older woman turned over cans of paint, looking for specific colors. She made noises of approval and disgust as she held each label up to the light, then set the ones she liked in the shopping cart next to her.

"So," Rhonda began, the tone in her voice trailing upward. "I noticed you and that Alex boy aren't sleeping in the same room."

Morgan almost laughed, setting out a single huff of breath. The statement had nearly been posed to her as a question, the passive aggressiveness offended her, and the randomness felt ridiculous.

"I'm sorry. What?" Morgan asked, allowing the woman the chance to restate her question.

"Well, you know. I saw the ring on your finger."

Morgan unconsciously grabbed her hand and covered up her ring, almost instinctively. Rhonda stared at her, studying Morgan's reaction.

"Oh," the leathery skinned woman said, her face looking like it cracked when she smiled. "Is there a problem?"

"I don't really want to talk about it," Morgan said, trying to be blunt about her annoyance.

"I understand. Of course," Rhonda said, acting as if she were going to go back to her search for just the right color when she stopped and turned back toward Morgan. "Oh! Wait! Is he not the one who gave you the ring?"

AFTER LIFE

Morgan stared at the bleached blond woman, a look of shock slapped across her face.

"Now don't get upset, I'm not judging you," Rhonda said. "I'm no angel. I'm just wondering how close you two are. I mean, did you just meet him?" She turned around, ignoring Morgan's unchanging face and continued looking through the paint. "Is he just someone to keep you warm at night?"

Morgan dropped the flashlight on the ground and walked away.

Rhonda's voice called after her, "And by the way, looking for pills in the pharmacy is useless, honey. We've picked it clean!"

Day 33

3:13 pm

Nathan, who was hooking up a fresh car battery to a generator, wiped off his hands and then crossed the room to sit down next to Alex on the plush couch. The man's sudden presence next to Alex hardly shook him from his trance. Alex barely reacted to Nathan, still staring off at the children on the floor.

"Alex?" Nathan finally said, announcing himself.

"Mm?" Alex said, drowsily turning his head toward the large man.

"I just, uh..." Nathan stumbled. "I just wanted to, you know, check in with you. See how everything has been going since you... I mean we haven't gotten a chance to really talk since..."

"It's okay," Alex smiled. He had been taken aback by the large man's demeanor ever since they arrived. His arms looked massive and cruel, nearly covered in dark black tattoos. His voice rumbled from deep in his belly. But the man had been nothing but calm and sensitive. Even the children were unafraid of him. "Everything has been fine. We have it pretty good here."

Nathan looked to the scattered individuals around the department. Some watched a DVD on the big screen TV, while others played cards.

"Yes we do," his voice purred with a slight twinge of something Alex didn't recognize.

Alex wished the man hadn't agreed. He desperately wanted to know that someone else felt uncomfortable with the falseness that surrounded them. He wanted to know someone else was unsettled by it and that he wasn't just rocking the boat.

"Where's your girlfriend?" Nathan asked, looking around the room.

"She's not my... I mean. I don't know. She wandered off somewhere."

"She's a good woman," Nathan said. "I can tell she has a good head on her shoulders."

"I know." Alex smiled.

"You guys..." Nathan held up his hand, "I mean, I'm not saying anything, I just... you don't seem very close."

Alex's eyebrows rose as he at looked at Nathan, curious what the large man was getting at. "Yeah, well, things have been sort of complicated between us."

"Complicated?"

"And a long story."

Nathan smiled, understanding Alex's unwillingness to talk. "Okay. I didn't mean to stick my nose where it don't belong. I just hate to see people unhappy when they... when they got something good."

"I appreciate your concern," Alex tried not to sound sarcastic. He did appreciate the man's empathy. "It's just not that simple."

"I guess I understand, but I just hope you aren't letting something that happened before all this stop you."

Alex let his mind wander, trying to place his emotions in a more vulnerable place, but the instinctual guards he had placed around his brain made it difficult. Everything in his body warned him not to feel. He let himself weaken for only a moment. He tried desperately to push it back again, feeling the onslaught approaching, but it was useless. The emotion he had stored away was so massive it dwarfed his defenses, making his body crumple under its weight. Almost instantly a tangled whirlwind of guilt and passion, hopelessness and love, came spinning into his body. It flushed tears from his eyes almost instantly.

"Whoa man." Nathan backed away, shocked at the reaction Alex had. "What did I say?"

"No, no." Alex sobbed. "It's not you. I'm so sorry. I just..."

Nathan set his giant hand on Alex's shoulder, enveloping it completely. The man's bare arms looked like tree trunks when they were that close, and Alex felt safe near his strength. He fought the urge to fall against the man and curl up into his arms, wanting badly to feel like a child again.

"It's going to be okay," Nathan said in a soft voice.

"I'm so scared, Nathan. I just... I just want to protect her and I don't know if I can."

"You've done a damn good job so far."

"Have I?" Alex asked, his eyes red from crying. "Have I really? I'm not sure anymore. I... I did some things that..."

"Alex, listen." Nathan voice became quiet, nearly whispering. "We've all done something. Every single person that is alive today has done something they aren't proud of. Or wouldn't be proud of in their old life. But that's why we're alive. That's why we survived when so many didn't. Because we were willing to do whatever it took to protect ourselves and the people we loved."

"I'm not sure I can live with what I did."

"Yes you can," Nathan said securely. "You have been."

Alex shook his head, "You don't understand."

Nathan grunted, silently trying to decide whether he should share his own story. With a heavy breath he rubbed his forehead and leaned back, letting his entire body relax.

"When they first locked the doors," Nathan began, "we all just stood by the glass, staring out at the murder that spilled across the parking lot. I saw men, and women, and even... even children. All getting devoured by blood covered corpses. I saw people pushing other people into the arms of their attackers, just so they could get away."

Nathan's head fell back and he stared up at the black ceiling covered in ventilation shafts.

"No one got away. No matter what they did and how many people they sacrificed. No one survived. At the time, I was appalled, like every one else. Horrified that humanity had resorted to caveman rules so quickly. Kill or be killed."

Nathan sat up straight and looked at Alex, accentuating his words.

"But then I looked at us. Were we any better? We sat back and watched it happen. Is our inaction any less evil than their actions?"

"You couldn't have helped them."

"No? Do you know that for sure?"

Alex paused and then shook his head.

"My wife. My unborn daughter. They live on the other side of town."

Nathan was staring at the floor now, unable to look into Alex's eyes as he spoke.

"Everyday I look outside and think 'today is the day.' Today is the day I will leave and I will find them, and I will be a hero because I faced insurmountable odds just to be with my family."

Alex saw tears rolling down Nathan's face. The imposing frame of the man melted away and his body began to fold under the weight of his thoughts.

"I never leave," he spoke, the tears now dripping off his lips. "I can never summon the bravery I need to go out there. I can never..."

Nathan shook his head, wiping his face with the back of his hand.

"I tell myself they're dead now. I tell myself they're dead so that I can sleep at night. I want them to be dead so that I made the right decision in staying."

Alex placed his hand on the man's shoulder and squeezed, saying, "No one blames you. I'm sure if your wife were-" He paused. "She would understand why you did what you did. She would want you to live."

"It doesn't matter," Nathan said, his posture suddenly stiffening. "I have to live with it now."

Alex watched the man's face. Nathan did not have the cold, stone, unfeeling face he expected. His face was one of pain. And acceptance. He truly was living with his decisions.

Unlike me.

Alex lowered the volume of his voice to nearly a mumble under his breath. "I let someone die. I let those things kill him so that... so that Morgan could live."

Nathan slowly turned and looked at Alex, asking with genuine concern, "Did you have a choice?"

"It didn't feel like it."

"You saved your girlfriend's life. You need to focus on that."

"Yeah," Alex said, trying to believe Nathan's logic. "She's not my..."

"Nathan!" Owen yelled from across the enclosed space. "Come here a second, will ya?"

Nathan nodded at Owen and patted Alex's leg as he stood up. He turned his head around and flashed Alex a smile before walking over to Owen who had Harold and Brenda standing near him.

As Alex watched Nathan lift boxes of car batteries onto a cart, he found himself uneasy. A knot began to form in his stomach again when he felt his mind try to push away his feelings. He still felt himself trying to bottle it up.

He stood up from the couch and stumbled off into the darkness. There he found a place where he could see nothing, even when his eyes were open. There he lost himself in his mind and openly wept. He allowed his mind to completely fall apart, to lie in ruins.

He knew he could rebuild.

He knew he would be stronger.

Day 39

6:26 pm

Morgan wandered into the clothing section of the store, looking for a clean t-shirt. When she got deep into the department, she heard Ashley and Emma laughing somewhere in the darkness. Morgan pointed her flashlight toward the noises. Near the corner of the dressing rooms, the two of them sat in overly fluffy prom dresses, tears streaming down their faces as their laughter was uncontrollable.
"What are you two doing?" she laughed, immediately jealous of their emotion.
The two girls were startled by Morgan's light and Morgan saw them both straighten up, trying to act "normal."
"Nothing," Ashley answered back. "Just trying on clothes."
"Sounds fun," Morgan said, stepping closer to them.
"Turn off your light, my Dad will see us," Emma said, her voice mumbling with a lisp. "And it's *so* bright…"

"What?" Morgan asked, sincerely confused.

"My Dad. I don't want him to come over here" Her words were slurred together.

Morgan shined the flashlight into Emma's face and saw her pupils rolling back into her head under barely open eyelids.

"What is wrong with you?" Morgan asked, stepping forward. "Were you guys drinking?"

"It's fine. She's fine," Ashley said, grabbing onto Morgan's arm and lowering the flashlight out of Emma's face.

"What's going on?" Morgan said seriously, looking into Ashley's eyes, which were also barely open, but looked straight forward.

"We just took some pills," Ashley answered, annoyed. "Nothing strong. We didn't even take that much."

Morgan's face remained unchanged, her reaction muted. "What did you take?"

"Oxycontin. It's fine. I've taken it before, I know what I'm doing."

Morgan's face continued its blankness. "You're getting high? When those things are outside?"

"Yeah. 'When those things are outside.' That's exactly the reason *why* I'm getting high."

"Ashley, you can't just-" Morgan began, but Ashley cut her off.

"I can't what? I can't try to forget about what's outside? I can't try to pass these days by without crying my eyes out with boredom? You should try it before you knock it."

"No Ashley, I just mean-"

"Just stop. You're not that much older than me. Don't act like you know any better what's going on."

Morgan was about to start yelling back at her, but caught her breath and let out a heavy sigh instead. "Ashley. You're… you're right. You can do anything you want to."

Morgan shook her head and readjusted her glasses. "I'm not judging you. It's just Emma. She's young."

"You can't tell me... tell me..." Emma's voice drifted off as her eyes rolled into her head again.

Morgan looked at Emma and felt nothing. Feeling no sympathy for the young girl in her pathetic state, Morgan knew she had completely turned off. Morgan sat down with them. Turning off her flashlight, she let her eyes adjust to the near darkness.

"When you stay here a few more weeks and you start to feel your brain melting from the monotony, let me know." Ashley leaned back. Morgan could hear the smile on her lips as she talked. "There's plenty of pills to go around."

Morgan said nothing. Her mind considered the place that small bottle of pills could take her. A place far away from here.

"Do you have any cigarettes on you?" Ashley asked.

Morgan tossed Ashley the rest of a crumpled up pack from her pocket. "I'm actually trying to quit."

"What?" Ashley was shocked by the concept. "Why in hell would you want to do that? Seems like a pretty merciful way to go now days."

Morgan shrugged her shoulders. "Yeah, I just... I don't know. I'm just..." Her face scrunched up in discomfort as she tried to change the subject awkwardly. "I haven't seen you around the group much."

"Yeah," Ashley mumbled, holding a cigarette in her lips while she dug in her pockets for her lighter. "That's sort of on purpose."

"Do you just not get along with them, or..." Morgan paused, trying to figure out exactly what she was asking.

Ashley let out a deep drag from her cigarette, smiling as she said, "What is this?"

"What?"

"Why are you asking me this? Why are you pretending to care?"

"Pretending? I'm not pretending. I was just asking you because…"

"Because why? Because you feel bad that I take pills to get through this bullshit? Because you think you can help me?"

"No," Morgan said gently, trying to be as genuine as possible. "I'm sorry. I didn't mean to… I understand about the pills. It's easier not to feel."

"Are you joking?" Ashley laughed. "I take that shit so that I *can* feel. Something other than this. Something other than pain, and misery, and hopelessness. I take that shit so that maybe, just maybe, I might find something to laugh at again."

Morgan was silent for a long pause.

"I'm sorry," Morgan finally said softly.

"Forget it," Ashley answered, blowing out another lung full of smoke forcefully.

"I feel like if I let myself feel anything, I'll break. Like I'm just going to shatter into a million pieces and scatter across the floor."

Ashley shrugged, not sure she completely understood Morgan's state, but knowing that she could relate. She sucked down a deep drag from her cigarette.

"What about Alex?" Ashley asked, her voice sharp and unsympathetic. "Aren't you two like totally in love, or whatever?"

"No. I mean, not really, but…" Morgan struggled to explain it to herself, much less anyone else. "Alex and I aren't really…" Morgan sighed, taking another pause to figure out the best word to use.

"How long have you guys been together?" Ashley asked, trying to help her focus her thoughts.

"We've been friends for years, but we aren't really 'together.' I mean, I am… I was…" Morgan nervously spun her engagement ring on her finger. "Someone asked me to marry them and it wasn't Alex, but I don't think my fiancé is..." Morgan took a deep breath. Speaking her thoughts out loud felt like finalizing them. Like signing a contract. Her voice would make it true.

"I don't think my fiancé is alive."

"You totally love Alex," Emma mumbled, almost tipping over even though she was sitting on the floor.

Ashley took a drag and let the smoke roll out her nose, burning the insides of her nostrils. "Do you?"

Morgan stared into the darkness. The dim glow coming from the electronics department barely gave her enough light to see Ashley's silhouette.

"I don't know if I can answer that."

"You don't know if you can... or *should*."

Morgan thought about the question. She let the concept roll around in her mind.

"It has barely been a month. I don't even know for sure that Christopher is dead."

"Christopher is your fiancé?"

"Yes," Morgan answered, her voice becoming weak.

"And so you think that it's not right that you're having these feelings for Alex."

"Right now? Honestly? It doesn't seem right to have any feelings." Morgan shifted in her chair and let out a sigh, assuring herself it was okay to speak. "My parents died. They died last year and when it happened, I was... I was so lost. I was looking for someone to blame and just trying to figure out why it happened, and I couldn't believe something so terrible had happened. I wanted them to be alive so badly."

Ashley was silent, smoking her cigarette and just letting Morgan talk.

"Now... now that all this has happened and I've seen everything that people have lived through, and when I see Alex worry about whether or not his mom lived, or his dad lived..." Morgan held her face in her hands, embarrassed by her words. "Now I'm happy my parents died. Now I'm happy they never had to see this. I'm happy I don't have to worry about what happened to them. I know they're dead. I know where they are and how it happened and that they died quickly and..." Her words were lost in a flood of tears. "I'm scared that I want Christopher dead too!"

Ashley felt an urge to comfort Morgan, but her baser instinct of coldness cut in and stopped her from moving. She stayed where she was and simply spoke.

"I think you're afraid to feel because things might change and you might be wrong again. You're afraid what you feel isn't what you're supposed to feel, and if you let yourself be with Alex... then that means Christopher is dead."

Morgan said nothing, too scared to admit the girl was right.

"What you need to realize," Ashley explained, letting out another drag of her cigarette as she spoke. Each word let out a small puff. "What you need to *accept*, is that the way you feel about Alex has nothing to do with Christopher. If you love Alex, it doesn't mean you were wrong about Christopher. It doesn't make the way you felt about him any less real."

Morgan was shocked at Ashley's maturity. "I just want it to be okay to be happy. Every time I almost say something to him, every time I almost tell him what I've always felt about him, every time I finally accept this new world, and that my old life is over, something reminds me..." She took slow breaths. "And then I turn off. Then I just go numb."

"You can't do that," Ashley said, her voice sounding deep and brooding. "If you turn off like that, you might as well be dead already."

"I want to feel..."

"Life is short, girl. Even shorter than when they used to say, 'life is short,'" Ashley said with a snarky tone.

"I know."

Morgan began to cry, feeling something for the first time in weeks.

Maybe years.

Her body shook, convulsing with each whimper. Her mind flushed through every painful memory she had held back and every denied emotion, releasing it all.

Ashley and Emma moved next to her, pushing her wet hair from her face and holding her. The three of them rocked back and forth, slowly.

AFTER LIFE

Day 39

8:02 pm

Alex – who sat in the electronics section with Owen, Harold, and Mr. Peterson playing cards – ignored everyone's protest to Herman Leblanc's choice of classical music for the night, and enjoyed the orchestral score. Alex knew their card game was slow and half-hearted, none of them particularly interested in who was winning. Days held nothing more than passing time.

Owen slapped down a king of hearts on the discard pile and said, "I wanted to run something by you fellas."

Harold picked up the king and traded it for one of his own cards. "What is it?"

"I've been talking to Nathan about this, but I thought I'd see how you guys feel." Owen cleared his throat and sat up straight. "What Alex told us about the military... it got me thinking. Thinking about Fort Ripley."

"The army base?" Mr. Peterson asked. "My cousin was stationed there when he was in the reserves."

"Really?" Owen perked up. "Do you know the way?"

"Sure." Harold asked, "Why?"

"I think that if the military is really out there, than we should try to contact them."

"Yes!" Harold shouted, slamming his fist on the table for effect. "Absolutely!"

Owen kept talking, trying to keep the momentum of the conversation. "Listen, if we can get to Fort Ripley, they might have a radio, or something we can use to get in touch with whoever it was that set off those bombs."

Mr. Peterson rubbed his chin, pondering the idea. Harold just kept nodding, looking back and forth at everyone else sitting at the table.

Alex shook his head again, not giving the idea much thought before he dismissed it. "I don't think it's worth the risk. If the military are really in any shape to fight back, they'll find us."

"You don't know that," Mr. Peterson said.

"And *you* don't know if they are even there," Alex said, arguing back at him. "We're safe. We have plenty of food. Why risk it?"

"It's important that we... we need to find other survivors," Owen said, lying his hand face down on the table. "Of course everything is fine here, but if the government is still active..."

"Absolutely," Mr. Peterson agreed. "The government."

Alex ignored Mr. Peterson. "You didn't hear the radio. I mean, they sounded like a bunch of kids playing with firecrackers. I don't think these guys are who you want them to be. Besides, we can't risk anyone's life on a hunch. The bombs they set off may have been their last idea. What if they gave up when it didn't work?"

Harold looked angry as he pointed his fat finger in Alex's face. "America's troops don't give up."

"Whoa." Alex held up his hands and slid his chair away from the table. "I didn't say anything about... I mean, come on, you aren't seriously going to pull that patriotic bullshit on me are you?"

Owen stood up and stepped behind Harold saying, "First of all, we don't need to use that kind of language. Second, I don't find anything wrong with 'patriotism,' Alex. This is America-"

"No!" Alex yelled, cutting him off, "This isn't America. Not anymore. There is no America. There is no military. At most they are people just like us, but with better weapons."

"You better watch your tongue," Harold said, his face turning red under his thick black beard.

"I'm telling you the truth. That's all. I just don't want anyone else to die needlessly."

Owen held his hand out, saying, "Alex, I think you better find somewhere else to take a time-out and cool off."

Alex stared into the falsely calm eyes of Owen, infuriated with him. His head felt as if it were swelling with blood before he finally exhaled and stomped away, cursing under his breath. As Alex walked away he heard Mr. Peterson and Owen begin talking about Mr. Peterson's willingness to leave the store to look for the base.

In the dark of the store Alex sat amongst the shelves of greeting cards. He stared at the floor, sunlight from the front doors giving him just a fraction of light. By his feet laid a card with a monkey in a dress on it and he was reminded of the ridiculousness of society before the infection. The same life so many people in the store wanted to hold onto.

"Is it someone's birthday?" Nathan's voice came from behind him, startling his perception of being alone.

Alex spun around and saw the large man smiling down at him.

"I heard you arguing with Owen," Nathan said, leaning against the shelf of cards.

"He said you didn't think it was a good idea either."

Nathan shrugged. "I don't. I tend to think you're right. Blowing up Minneapolis doesn't make me feel like we're winning."

"I swear, it only took a few minutes for them to be walking around again. Most of them got blown apart, and the ones that didn't were pretty damaged, but as soon as you left the blast zone-"

"I believe it," Nathan said, shaking his head as he stared at the floor. "I mean this isn't a normal war. Who the hell knows how to kill something that's already dead?"

"Time," a voice from near the cash registers called out.

Nathan spun around and shined his flashlight on the spot where the sound came from. In the light he saw Brenda, the high school science teacher, holding an arm full of candy bars.

"Sorry, I couldn't help but overhear," Brenda said, looking embarrassed. "I was just... I have a sweet tooth and Rhonda rations out the chocolate like a Nazi and I found some chocolate and hid it away up here. Which I guess I have to move now that you know."

"It's okay," Nathan stopped her.

"What did you mean?" Alex asked. "You said 'time.'"

"Well, I mean, just look at them out there," Brenda said, walking toward Nathan and Alex. "The early summer and humid days aren't doing them any favors. A corpse left out to the elements, it can be almost completely decayed in a little over a month."

"But those things, they aren't regular corpses," Nathan said, his voice a paranoid whisper.

"Oh sure they are," Brenda nearly laughed. "Don't tell me you believe this annoying hybrid of Christianity and Voodoo that the media was preaching? I mean, listen, I went to church every Sunday. The difference is I believe God uses science to perform his miracles."

"So you believe this is a virus?" Alex asked.

"A virus? That's the most likely. Remember that bad outbreak we had a few years ago of smallpox?"

"Sure," Nathan answered. "I was out of work for almost a month."

"Well, luckily, it was the minor strain, right?" Brenda talked with her hands, obviously used to illustrating her points to groups of people. "Or at least that's what they told us. What if this was a new strain? What if the second phase of the virus didn't show up till now?"

"The second phase?"

"Well, most people get chicken pox when they're kids, right? In a few people, the virus reactivates years later. That's what causes shingles."

"So wait," Nathan tried to clarify. "You're saying that the small pox we had stayed in our bodies and just now decided to start waking us up when we die?"

"Well..." Brenda chuckled. "I wouldn't put it quite like that. I mean, I would never claim to understand what's happening, but..."

"If you had to guess," Alex said, trying to urge her on.

"If I had to guess? I suppose it's possible that the virus laid dormant in our nervous system and recently reactivated. When it senses death it moves to the brain and stimulates minor functions. Hunger, aggression... nothing more than slightly advanced convulsing." Brenda scratched her head. "It makes sense, but this is all just a guess."

"They're just bodies." Alex smiled, comforted by the thought.

"Of course," Brenda laughed, "What did you think... they were zombies?"

Day 42

12:10 am

The beam from the flashlight shot out from the make shift bathroom fence where Alex pulled aside the green tarp. He and Morgan peered through the chain link into the parking lot.

They spoke in whispers.

"Did she seem positive?"

"No. Not completely, but it makes sense. First they started slowing down. Then they started decaying. Now look at them."

"I'm not saying I don't believe her."

Alex reached out and placed his hand on Morgan's shoulder as he said, "We could leave. Tomorrow. These things wouldn't even pose much of a threat. We'd just have to keep our eyes out for fresh ones."

"Fresh ones," Morgan said with a shiver.

"As long as we had a car, I don't think we'd be in much danger," Alex said, trying to assure her. "We'll just have to find gas as we go."

Morgan kept staring out the fence, saying, "Are you sure we should leave this place? I mean, we're safe and..."

"Yes. I'm sure," Alex said bluntly. "This place is like one big fake life. Everyone is just hanging on to what they used to be. The sooner we leave, the better. I don't want to still be here when the batteries and the food run out and these people are forced to realize what the world has become."

Morgan nodded, slowly walking away from the fence. Alex peeked out one last time, watching a corpse trip and fall over, then struggle to stand back up. He jogged away from the fence and caught up with Morgan.

"I need you to be sure you want to do this," Alex said, his voice almost sounding whiny.

"Alex. If we do this, you need to know something."

Alex looked at Morgan in the darkness, her face barely lit by the flashlight pointed at the ground. She looked blank and her ghost-like personality scared him. Her lips parted and the words curled from them like smoke. They escaped into the air and were tossed by a breeze.

"I'm pregnant."

Alex stopped. Morgan took a few more steps before turning and reluctantly looked into his flashlight. His mouth kept opening, like he was about to speak, but he never made a noise.

"I just found out. I mean I think I kind of knew for a while, but I finally took a pregnancy test."

Alex continued to try to speak, but did little more than grunt before sucking in his breath and then trying to say something else.

"I'm going to keep it, if that's what you're wondering. It's... it's..."

"It's beautiful."

Morgan smiled a bit when she saw the innocent look on Alex's face. "Do you still think we should leave?"

"What? Of course! More so!"

"I was afraid you'd think it was too dangerous."

Alex smiled. "What *isn't* dangerous now days. Besides, we need to. I mean maybe we can find a doctor... or something."

"Even without one, I'm sure we'll be fine." Morgan nodded a single time to solidify how she felt. "People have been having babies for a long time. Long before there were hospitals, and drugs, and whatever else."

Alex stepped forward and hugged her, saying, "Congratulations."

They stood there, in the middle of Wal-Mart, holding each other. Alex squeezed harder, letting her know he was there. She let her chin fall against his shoulder.

"I'll take care of you both," Alex said.

"And we'll both take care of you," she mumbled, her lips pressing into his shirt.

AFTER LIFE

Day 42

8:49 am

Morgan woke up in Alex's room, curled up in a sheet on his bed. She rubbed her eyes and looked around, finding Alex lying in a fetal position on the floor. She remembered talking with him, late into the night. An honest talk. A vulnerable talk. Whispers that were more intimate than kisses.

Morgan nudged Alex gently, leaning down close to him so that the first thing he would see was her smiling face. His eyes fluttered open, a confused look crushing his eyebrows together. As his vision cleared and her smile came into view, his face relaxed.

"Is it morning already?"

"It is," Morgan said. "I just want to get this over."

He sat upright, sucking in a deep breath. "Yeah. Okay. You're right. The sooner we get going, the more daylight we'll have."

Morgan and Alex straightened themselves out and left the bedroom, walking toward the sounds of breakfast.

"Okay. So, we'll tell them, then collect supplies, and whatever they can spare for food."

"Are we going to see if anyone wants to come with?" Morgan asked.

"I'm still not sure. I mean, Nathan seems like a good person and I feel responsible for Emma for some reason."

"Herman seems okay, too. Probably Ashley."

"See, I just don't know how we would only offer the opportunity to some of the survivors and not all of them."

Morgan shrugged. "I doubt Owen would even want to come with. He's pretty damn happy here."

The topic trailed off as they neared the electronics department, an air of secrecy following them. When they stepped between the shelves bordering the department the entire group that sat at the table hushed themselves and turned to look at Morgan and Alex.

"Alex! Morgan! Good morning!" Owen called out, his thin smile breaking open as he stood from the table.

Alex watched Nathan stand up after Owen, flashing a strange look in Alex's direction before walking to the outskirts of the department.

"I've been eager to talk to the both of you," Owen said as he was suddenly at their side, gripping onto Alex's arm and leading them to the table.

"Yeah," Alex said. "We wanted to talk to you, too."

"Oh good, oh good. Why don't we all have a seat at the table and talk then." Owen held out his hand, presenting an open seat in front of him.

Alex was disturbed by the looks on everyone's faces, but mindlessly sat down, noticing only once he was seated, that Nathan had made his way behind him. The large man now stood in the background with his arms crossed.

"What's going on?" Morgan directed the question at Owen, but looked around the table, hoping for anyone to offer an answer.

"We've been talking, all of us, about the Army base. Fort Ripley. We decided, as a group, that it's a good idea."

"Um, okay." Alex was frightened now. He had no idea what was happening. He noticed that Emma and Ashley were gone. Mr. Peterson looked quieter than usual. He almost looked defeated. "Did you talk about-"

"We discussed it at length," Owen assured him. He placed his hand on Morgan's shoulder and Alex could hear Nathan behind him moving closer to them. "In fact, we talked about it a long time ago"

Alex was even more confused now.

"We tried to talk you into it. We wanted you to go along with us willingly."

Alex looked up at Nathan who stared him down with a look like cold stone.

He turned his gaze back to Owen before saying, "Owen! Wait. I don't know what is going on, but it doesn't matter what I think. Do whatever you want. Morgan and I are leaving."

"You're half right," Owen said and then nodded at Nathan.

The large, dark skinned man with the massive tattoo covered arms leapt forward, his hands clasping down on Alex's shoulders, his weight pinning Alex's shocked body to the chair. Alex screamed out as Owen helped Harold get a good grip on Morgan with his chubby fingers.

Alex's survival instinct kicked in. His body began convulsing in the chair, doing anything he could to break free from Nathans giant grip.

"What are you doing?" Alex growled at Nathan, shocked at the man's complete change in demeanor.

"Now just settle down," Owen said more to Alex, but he held out his hand to the cringing members of the group. It wasn't until then that Alex realized the children were gone. Brenda was gone too. Rhonda was almost grinning behind Owen.

They had planned this.

"Let's just talk this out, okay?" Owen offered, clasping his hand together in front of him.

"Let her go Owen," Alex growled again. "Let her go or I *will* kill you."

Owen let out a dramatic sigh. "I told you folks. I told you he would act like this. Fine. We gave it a shot. Gary? Hand me the rope."

AFTER LIFE

Day 43

1:08 am

The break-room had no light in it, causing the darkness to surround Alex. He struggled against the coarse rope wrapped around his wrists, his arms bloody from the friction. Both his arms and ankles were tied to a metal table that was heavy enough to make it impossible for him to move. His arms hadn't stopped flexing since they tied him down and the rope had dug deep into his skin. A pool of blood formed on the floor below him, but his teeth ground the pain away as he focused his attention on the door across the room, summoning every ounce of his strength to break free from his bonds.

He screamed with anger when he pictured the men tying up Morgan. He had jumped across the table at them, unafraid at that moment of any consequence, but was struck down by Nathan's massive fist slamming him between the eyes. He could feel the lump that had swelled across the bridge of his nose.

He woke up here, feeling the ropes binding him as he regained consciousness, his body still fueled with adrenalin. He could hear Owen talking once and awhile outside the door, but it was never close enough to hear. Simply a murmur in the darkness. Other than that one noise, it was just him, staring at a point in the black.

He screamed out again, ready to explode with anger.

No one would hurt her. He promised her she would survive. She carried a child. She was his purpose in life. She was his everything.

Everything.

As hours of struggling stretched on, the adrenalin in his body wore off and he felt weak, folding in on himself while cold sweat ran down his back. He slumped to one side, the ropes on his wrists the only thing holding his body upright. His blood and sweat pooled together below him. His body told him to cry, but he turned his sadness into anger, forming a straight line to Owen in his mind.

He was startled back into consciousness, having no way of knowing how much time had passed in the pitch black. What woke him was the door to the break-room slamming open. Owen walked in with Harold right behind him, carrying a large flashlight. Owen had his sleeves rolled up to his elbows and his hair looked messy. Even though the old man had no smile on his face and looked quite serious, Alex could tell he was happy.

Owen walked straight at Alex and punched him in the face. Alex was shocked and unready for the hit. His eyes swelled up in pain. His nose felt crooked.

"I figured we might as well get that out of the way," Owen said. "And besides, I've been looking forward to it."

Alex spit on the floor and tasted the iron flavor of blood.

"Now, I want to offer you the deal one more time before we do anything," Owen said, rubbing the hand that he used to punch Alex. "I hope you take this. I really do. Everything will go so much more simply."

Owen grabbed a chair and sat down in front of Alex, only feet away from him. Alex strained against the ropes, praying he could burst free and strangle the man in front of him.

"We want you to go to Fort Ripley," Owen said. "With Mr. Peterson. Just go there and see what you can see. If someone is there, you just tell them where we are. If no one is there, you grab what you can and bring it back. No one gets hurt."

"Where's Morgan?" Alex spit the words through blood that was dripping from his nose. "Just let me leave with her. You'll never see us again."

Owen punched him again, this time his fist landed squarely on Alex's left eye. His head rocked back and then rolled forward. He was shocked at the power in the old man's fist.

"Now Alex, you aren't listening." Owen sounded like he was feigning annoyance. "Let me try to explain this."

Owen cleared his throat. He lashed out with his other hand, catching Alex across the jaw, before saying, "We knew about the army before you got here. For a while before they set off those bombs, we heard them on the radio."

Owen leaned back and looked at Harold who stood perfectly still next to the door, holding the flashlight. The old man said to Harold as much as to Alex, "We all sort of agreed that we had to go there and let them know about us, but none of wanted to risk our own lives."

"You piece of shit." Alex moaned in pain. "What makes you think I would risk my life for you?"

"Well honestly, for awhile I was afraid nothing would convince you. I was fairly certain Mr. Peterson would take the trip for Emma. Even a hard ass like him doesn't want to see his own daughter die." Owen's eyebrows raised high above his eyes. "But then Nathan got you to open up about Morgan."

"You bastard. You were going to hold Morgan and Emma for ransom?" Alex's words fumbled from swollen lips. "No. No, I'll kill you! I'm telling you, I will kill you if you even touch her."

Owen shook his head, before punching Alex again and saying, "I don't even think you know what you're fighting against anymore. You were happy when you got here. I fed you and put clean clothes on you and all I'm asking you to do is to prove to me that you deserve a share of our food. Of our electricity."

"You're insane, Owen."

Owen lashed out with his fist again, but Alex's face now tingled with numbness.

Owen hooked his fist around again and brought it smashing into Alex's cheek, screaming, "You little punk. How dare you judge me. How dare you! You have no clue what I'm doing. You have no idea what kind of madness is in this world."

"I do now, Owen," Alex said before spitting more blood on the floor, his eyes swelling so much he could barely see.

Owen hit him again. And again.

"You have no idea what you're throwing away." Owen started to walk around behind Alex as he said, "Humans cannot handle this much loss and not be affected by it. We have enough supplies to maintain at least a fragment of what we used to be. I was trying to give you something that at least resembled what you knew. I want to make the transition as easy as possible. I don't want to forget who we were while it happens."

"The transition? To what? The end of the world? That is happening right now! That happened a month and a half ago! You can't just ignore it until you're ready to deal with it! Do you really think that's what people need now?

AFTER LIFE

Do you really think getting our cable TV back is the most important thing?"

"I don't need to argue with you," Owen said as he circled back around Alex, stopping in front of him. "If you refuse to do this, then I'll let Harold here kill you."

"You can't even do it yourself. You're pathetic."

"No," Owen said calmly. "I'm not going to be killing anyone. No one will trust me with blood on my hands, and if I'm going to lead this group, I need them to trust me. But I can't let you live. I'll never be able to trust you. After you see what I'm going to do to Morgan, you'd never let it go..."

"I'll kill you!" Alex screamed wildly, "I'll kill you!"

Owen nodded at Harold and then walked out the door. He called out from the hallway, "When you're done, make sure to destroy the brain."

Harold stepped up to Alex, brandishing the uselessly large knife he had when Alex had first seen him. The man twisted the knife in the air and looked closely at its tip.

"You dumb shit, you shoulda just taken his offer," Harold said, his black beard making his face appear invisible in the darkness. "All this cause you hadda be a prick. Hadda go rockin the boat."

"Fuck you," Alex said, so separated from the reality of the situation that he felt no fear. His heartbeat was calm.

"Tell you what," Harold said, smiling a disgusting grin. "When I'm done with you..." He leaned in close to Alex's head and whispered into his ear, "I'll take care of your girlfriend for you."

Alex's body was flushed with emotion, his anger turned into pure, unflinching rage. His eyes enlarged with the white, hot fury that burst from his lungs. He released a scream so feral and animal-like that the walls in the room shook in terror. His mouth stretched open with the scream and Harold's head lunged to the side, allowing Alex to sink his teeth into Harold's neck. Veins twisted and broke between his teeth. Blood flushed into his mouth, making the muscle he bit in to slippery. He dug his teeth in as deep as he could and clenched them closed, tearing his face away with streams of Harold's neck hanging from his mouth.

Alex's ear rang with deafness from the squeal that Harold had shrieked inches from his head. Alex watched the man fall to the ground, dropping the knife as he reached for his neck, trying uselessly to stop the spray of red fluid that gushed from the opening. Alex spit out the hunk of flesh in his mouth and started wrenching his body to the side, hoping he could reach the knife on the seat next to him.

"You... little shit..." Harold managed to say, blood spitting up from his mouth with every word. His breath gurgled in the liquid. "You fucking killed me... you..." Harold fell to the ground, blood still spewing from the broken veins, collecting in a large pool under the still body.

Alex struggled harder, letting the rope dig deeper into his arms, the tips of his fingers touched the knife handle and he managed to spin it a bit closer. His eyes flashed between the knife and the body on the ground. The body that he now saw start to twitch. His hand inched closer up the hilt as he bent each finger at the knuckle, trying to pull the blade closer to him. Harold's arm started to flop around in the blood, splattering the thick fluid across the floor. Alex got his finger around the handle and pulled it closer, trying to flip the blade upright so he could slice it against the rope. Harold's head lifted from the floor, his beard drenched in blood and his lifeless eyes staring straight ahead. Alex pushed the blade up and down, feeling the fibers of the rope split underneath, slowly. Harold's head turned toward Alex and he let out a hissing scream, causing more blood to spray from his neck. His arms reached out as he tried to stand up in the slippery pool of blood. He reached for Alex, but fell over trying to right his awkwardly moving body. As Harold stood up and leaned forward, his teeth starting to gnash the air as he leaned in toward Alex, the rope around Alex's wrists broke free. Alex brought the knife up in a tight stab, smashing the tip of the blade into Harold's jaw, driving the wide blade up through his mouth and then deep into his brain.

Harold's lifeless body fell to its knees and then forward, dropping Harold's skewered head right in Alex's lap. With a quick shove the body fell to the ground and Alex began wrenching the blade from out of Harold's skull. After bracing the head against the floor, he yanked the blade out. He then cut his legs free and started tiptoeing toward the door. He counted in his head how many men he was about to kill.

I would kill the world if it meant she would live.
I would kill them all.

JARON LEE KNUTH

Day 43

1:53 am

The blade felt heavy, yet solid in Alex's hand. He kept his flashlight turned off, inching along the wall of the hallway, toward the direction of the main doors that led out into the electronics department. He inched closer to the managerial offices until he saw the flare of a flashlight beam flicker out the window on one of the doors. He flattened himself against the wall and stepped closer to the door, slowly.

He heard someone mumble something, then heard a *smack*. Like a fist hitting flesh. He leaned into the doorway, peeking around the corner through his swelled eye.

In the middle of the room, Morgan was tied to an office chair. Her arms and legs each tied to a leg of the metal furniture. With a leather belt in his hand was Jesse the toothless man, walking around her in a circle.

"Bet you scared now, eh girlie?" Jesse said this in a sinister whisper. "Bet yer hopin yer boyfriend takes the deal, huh?" Jesse struck out with the belt, whipping Morgan's back. Her shirt was covered in slashes, her skin broken open by the vicious lashings.

Alex, suddenly struck with a surge of fearlessness, stepped into the room, walking confidently toward Jesse. The toothless, skinny man was shocked for a moment and raised his arm so he could bring his belt down to strike Alex. Alex reached up, grabbing Jesse's arm with his left hand and stabbing the large knife into Jesse's stomach with his right hand.

Jesse's eyes bulged from his head when he looked down and he saw the blood flowing from his stomach. Alex only held the knife there for a moment, yanking it out and stabbing it back in, over and over.

Jesse fell to the floor silently, too shocked to even scream. The last breath fell from his body as Alex brought the knife down, crushing Jesse's skull under the massiveness of the blade.

"Alex?" Morgan mumbled, her voice sounding shattered.

"It's me." His words sounded weak and awkward through his swollen lips. His fingers shook as he tried to be gentle with her ropes. He did not want to inflict any more pain upon her.

"Alex. Thank you."

"What did they-" He knew he did not want to know.

When he freed her arms they immediately wrapped around her stomach and she crouched over, tightening the grip she held on herself and her unborn child.

Her voice quivered, each letter of each word making her tone flutter. "They just kept hitting me. They hit my belly."

Alex reached out his hand and placed it on Morgan's head. He let his fingers wrap around on all sides. One of her arms reached up and she grabbed his wrist. With a tug she pulled his hand down onto her belly.

"I'm going to save you. I'm going to save you both."

"Alex, you don't need to save us."

His heart tried to believe her. His mind wanted revenge.

"Let's sneak out the emergency doors in the back," Morgan said, lifting herself off the chair. "We can sneak around the building and find a car." Her face was swollen and plump, her skin broke open in gouges and cuts that would leave a permanent scar.

Alex looked down at the knife in his hand. The blade was jagged and still dripped with blood. He wanted to cut the smile off of Owen's face.

Morgan's hand lay gently on Alex's hand that gripped the knife so tightly. His face, still covered in the blood of Harold's neck, looked up into her eyes, which soothed the pain in his mind. The look she gave him, one of pure weakness, showed him something inside her that she rarely exposed to anyone. The soft, inner child that desperately needed his strength. The woman that was frightened and wanted only to turn and run. The beaten and frail person that needed to fall into his arms and weep.

"What about-"

"Forget them," Morgan said, her eyes sharp with intensity. "Forget all of them. It's me and you. Me and you."

"And me," a voice said from the doorway, its shape silhouetted behind a bright flashlight. Alex knew the voice. The soft, warm voice that boiled hatred inside him.

"Owen."

Owen slid the slide action of the shotgun Alex had brought with, loading a round in the chamber, ready to fire. He took two steps into the room, showing no fear of Alex, or Morgan.

"You couldn't just go along with the plan, could you?" His voice dropped all pretenses of his grandfatherly ways. There was simply spite and anger dripping from his teeth. "You couldn't just let us be happy?"

"Is that what you call this?" Morgan's mouth bled with pain. "How long did you really think this was going to last?"

"Long enough," Owen said, raising his shotgun. "And it will continue. Without you."

"No," Alex growled, lunging at the old man.

The gun lifted up and Owen pulled the trigger instinctively as Alex wrapped his fingers around the end of the barrel. The blast of the gun rocked the walls of the room, deafening Alex. The shell only grazed his side. Alex pushed the gun away from him and brought his knife up at Owen's chest. Owen fell backwards and the blade sliced along him, opening his flannel shirt and digging into his flesh.

Alex tried to wrestle the gun away from Owen, but he refused to loosen his grip. Alex slashed out again, this time the blade dug deep into the old man's shoulder. Owen yelped out in pain and then pulled the shotgun close to him so that the barrel once again pointed at Alex. With a quick jerk of the slide, another round was chambered and Owen pulled the trigger. The blast tore apart Alex's leg and he fell backwards, his hand letting go of the barrel.

Owen brought the gun up, ready to unleash another blast into Alex when he felt a leather belt wrap around his neck. The leather tightened suddenly and his neck began to bleed from the pressure, the air trapped in his lungs began to push at the walls of his chest.

He brought the shotgun up into the air and then lunged backwards with his elbow, trying to slam it into his attacker. Morgan simply pulled the belt tighter. Owen began to hack, drool spilling from his mouth. He chambered another round and Morgan gripped harder onto the belt. She slammed her knee into his spine and pushed down on Owen's back. He fell to the floor, the shotgun spinning across the office tile.

Owen continued spitting, as more and more blood joined his saliva on the floor in front of his face. His head filled with pressure and soon the old man fell slack, consciousness slipping away.

Morgan only let go of the belt when she heard Alex groan as he tried to stand up.

"Are you-" She managed to get out as she rushed to his side.

"I'm okay." He was wrapping Jesse's shirt around his leg. It looked bad. "I just... we need to get out of here. They must of heard the gunshots."

Morgan looked up when she heard a scream come from the hallway. There, standing in the doorway of the office, was Rhonda, Harold, and Gary. They started to move toward Owen when Morgan leaned down and picked up the shotgun, raising the barrel at their chests.

"Get out of our way," she said, her voice sounding like it rumbled from deep within her.

The group in the hallway did not move.

She lowered the barrel, pointing it at the now twitching body of Owen. With a tug of the trigger, the shotgun flattened his entire head against the floor, turning Owen's face into nothing more than a thin splatter.

The group stepped back, gasping.

Morgan chambered another round and kept the gun trained on all of them as she made her way out of the office. Alex kept close to her, dragging his leg behind.

The group of survivors whispered to each other as Morgan and Alex made their way into the front of the store, near the electronics department. With shrill screams, Morgan made them stand together, so she could keep her eyes on all of them. Some of them discharged curses at the two of them, while others begged for forgiveness.

Alex and Morgan heard nothing.

Even the looks of fear on the children's faces did nothing to move them. They only thought of each other.

Slowly Alex found gauze for his leg and began collecting supplies, while Morgan kept the shotgun pointed at the group. It took him a long time to move about the store, but Morgan did not mind. She glared into the eyes of all the people willing to hurt her. To hurt Alex. To hurt her baby.

She pictured each one, dying at the end of her barrel.

Alex finally gathered up four backpacks, stuffed with goods. By now, the survivors had learned the futility of their arguments and were saying nothing.

Morgan and Alex made their way to the front of the store. Alex slowly climbed the wall of shelves while Morgan kept watch. When he reached the top, Morgan tossed the gun to him and began to ascend. None of the men and women they had been living with sprung from the darkness to stop them.

The parking lot was still filled with corpses, but only a few were still able to move. Even those still upright only staggered and shuffled their way through the debris, barely able to match the speed of the one-legged Alex.

Morgan ran in between the cars, looking in each one and checking the doors, trying to find ones that was unlocked. Once and awhile she was forced to swing the stock of the shotgun at a corpse's head before moving on.

It took her a few minutes, each one creeping on longer than the last. Alex felt a sinking feeling with each car she passed. She would walk away from each one, holding up her hands to show there was no way to start it. Seeing this over and over, he began to lose hope.

Finally, her hands tossed into the air and she ran across the lane to a small red pick-up truck. She fumbled with something in the door and then held up her hand to show keys.

"They were still in the door," she yelled before swinging her shotgun and clobbering another zombie.

Alex hobbled across the parking lot and caught up to her as she was climbing into the driver's seat. He lifted himself into the passenger seat and slammed the door, biting his lip with anxiety as she turned the key.

The engine sputtered and died. He watched a group of corpses start to gather around the car. She turned the key again, this time stomping on the gas. The engine roared to life, revving powerfully with every press of the gas.

"Half of a tank," she said, dropping the gear shift into reverse.

The truck whipped out of the parking spot, knocking over two walking corpses that had gathered near the back. Morgan put the truck in drive and stomped on the gas, knocking over body after body as they sped straight toward the exit.

When the truck turned onto US-8, she let off the gas, bringing the vehicle to a slower pace. Alex looked down at his bloody leg and knew he would need to replace the bandage soon. He wasn't sure how much blood he had lost, but he knew it was too much. He pushed the shotgun out of the way and slid across the bench seat in the truck cab. He set his head on Morgan's shoulder and watched the sun start to rise in front of them.

Alex said in a whisper next to her ear, "We survived."

AFTER LIFE

Day 43

8:37 am

On the road in front of the truck the summer day was almost welcoming, with streets fairly clear of bodies and only the random need to circumvent an abandoned vehicle. The truck skimmed down the highway, letting wind into the open windows that blew Morgan's hair around uncontrollably. She leaned back in her seat and let her hair get tossed around, accepting it as beautiful chaos. A flock of birds dashed into the air as the truck roared close to them on the highway, and the sky was suddenly black with wings, causing Morgan to feel guilty for disturbing their nature.

The road trip was absent of speech, Alex and Morgan simply held hands across the seat and stared at the world around them, marveling in the beauty of its emptiness. The sun embraced the naked world.

Dusk drew near as the truck entered the town Alex's parents who now lived in Wausau, Wisconsin. The streets of the small town were empty except for the occasional pile of decayed flesh and bones. Newspapers blew across the pavement like tumbleweeds.

Morgan pulled up to the apartment building that Alex's mother had moved into after the divorce. Windows were open on every floor, some broken. Corpses littered the stairs leading to the front door of the building.

"I'm coming with you," Morgan said, matter-of-factly.

"I know you are," Alex said, squeezing her hand in his. They both climbed out of the truck, Morgan holding the shotgun and Alex carrying a flashlight.

"Don't shoot unless you have to," he reminded her as they both stepped into the dark building.

Alex turned on the flashlight and the beam cut down the hallway. His leg seized with pain every time he stepped down on it, but his mind pushed him forward. He stepped slowly, crunching debris under each footstep, walking carefully toward his mother's apartment.

His heart sank when he saw the door hanging open.

The inside looked like most interiors now looked. Dried blood splattered randomly throughout the house. Decayed corpses that were impossible to identify.

In her bedroom, he found a pile of bones strung together with dry flesh, dressed in a flannel nightgown he knew was hers. His eyes wanted to cry, so he let them, releasing the pain of not knowing her fate. She was curled up on her bed, looking somewhat peaceful. He tired to imagine what happened, but turned away, accepting he would never know.

"Let's go." He sniffled, wiping his nose with the back of his sleeve.

"Alex. I'm sorry," Morgan said, leaning into hug him.

He accepted her embrace, assuring her, "I know. I know."

AFTER LIFE

The truck weaved its way through the town and out onto the country road his father's house was on.

"Are you ready for this?" Morgan asked, her voice quiet.

Alex didn't answer, but continued to stare straight ahead while she drove. The silence was not as deafening as it used to be. She could see in his face. The turning of gears, not the blank stare she had almost gotten used to.

When the truck pulled into the driveway and around the large tree that sat in the front yard, hiding the front of the house, Alex saw his father's door broken in. Morgan gasped, sympathetic to the double pain Alex now felt. She could see the fear and failure of defeat in his eyes as the tears forming in them sparkled in the sunlight. She pressed on the brake and moved the gear into park. She lifted her hand to turn the key and turn off the engine, but Alex's hand shot out and stopped her.

"Leave it running, I'll just be a minute."

Morgan, about to protest, understood what Alex needed to do and sunk back into her seat, silently accepting his demand.

She watched him grab the shotgun and slide out of the cab. He hobbled on one leg, up the stairs, and entered the house. Only moments later she heard a single shot. Alex walked back out of the house and crawled into the cab of the truck.

"They're both gone."

Morgan nodded, "They're at peace now Alex."

Alex leaned over, whimpering into Morgan's chest, as she kissed the top of his head. She held him for a while before he collected himself and she put the truck into reverse, backing out of the driveway. They continued on for a few miles, before coming across a car dealership when their gas tank was nearly empty. They both searched the building, staying close, but never hearing anything resembling a moan. Every corpse lay in taters on the ground, unable to move. In the managers office they found a master set of keys and walked out into the lot, searching for the perfect car. Alex allowed himself to smile as they shopped.

When they finally chose a new car, with a full tank of gas, they drove down a nearby dirt road, looking for a place to stay for the night. It didn't take them long to find a small house, far from any neighbors. The house appeared to be a summer cabin for an upper middle class family and not lived-in during the outbreak. A small lake was behind the cabin. All the doors and windows still appeared secure.

Breaking one of the windows, they both crawled in and did a thorough search of the house before moving the entertainment center in front of the window they broke. They started a fire in the fireplace and cooked a small meal, neither of them very hungry. They both felt calm and moved through their actions sluggishly. When they curled up on the plush couch, watching the flames dance across the wood, slowly consuming it, inch by inch, they began to make plans.

They talked about heading back into Minnesota and visiting the Mayo Clinic. Alex not only felt there was a good chance of people surviving in a facility like that, but if they did, there was a good chance that there would be a doctor amongst the survivors.

Just then, Morgan felt a kick inside of her. The first movement she had felt since they left the Wal-Mart.

"It moved!" Her eyes, covered in tears, were glittering in the firelight. "My baby. My baby is alive."

He held onto her belly with a firm grip. The child inside of her was Christopher's child, but he was unmoved by this. He had already sworn his protection so many times that in his mind he was solely responsible for the child's safety.

He would love the child.

Just like he loved Morgan.

Alex laid his head on Morgan's belly and she watched his face in the fading sunset streaming through the

AFTER LIFE

window. She felt her chest rise, then fall with his. She felt all three of their hearts beat together.

JARON LEE KNUTH

Day 2378

Alex walked over a small hill, looking down on the field next to their house. He stood near hanging sheets on a clothes line, the white billowing against the long green grass.

Morgan was at the bottom of the hill, carrying a basket of freshly picked tomatoes from the garden to their house, and Alex's stomach growled when he thought about the way they tasted fresh from the plant.

As he lifted his gaze he saw the smokestacks of a factory in the distance, towering into the air, covered in vines. The sky above them was a vibrant blue. Birds flocked overhead. Past their fields he saw one of his neighbors eating lunch with his family at a table in their backyard. He was hesitant about living so close to someone again. There was always a chance that one of them could die and turn into a freshly animated corpse.

It was Morgan who finally talked him into it. She told him they needed to start trusting again. She said everyone was dangerous, even her. And that we would have to adjust to that. It was part of life now. It was part of death. He made a mental note to bring some tomatoes to his neighbors later in the day.

"Papa," a small voice erupted from behind him.

"Zoe." Alex smiled large under his thick beard, opening his arms to catch his daughter running at him. "Did you help Mom with the buckets?"

"Yup." The little girl nodded, crossing her eyes as she tried to see her own tongue, which was sticking straight out. "I carried one all by myself, too!"

"I don't doubt it," Alex said, pinching the girl's tiny arms. "These things are getting bigger every day!"

"Aw, Dad." The girl blushed. "What are you doing up here? All by yourself."

"I'm just admiring... *everything*. The world."

"What does that mean? 'Admiring?'"

"It means I'm looking at the world and I'm... I'm happy with what I see, and I'm thinking about why it makes me happy. I'm really stopping to notice how I feel."

"Oh." The girl nodded her head. "You do that with Mommy a lot."

Alex laughed from deep in his belly. "You're right, I do."

"So, why are you happy?"

"Well..." Alex sat down on the grass next to her so they were looking eye to eye. "Do you mean besides the obvious answer that's standing next to me?" They both laughed as he playfully dug his finger into her belly button.

"Besides me!" she squealed, trying to push his hand away.

"Okay, besides you." His tone became serious as he looked out across the rolling hills that surrounded them. "I'm happy because when I look at the world, I know it's going to be okay. I know that people can't hurt it anymore. Even if we wanted to, there just isn't enough of us. That makes me think that everything turned out okay. It makes me think that maybe this was the plan all along. Maybe everything is better off."

"I don't understand," the little girl said, shrugging her shoulders.

"I know. And that makes me happy too."

"You're happy I don't understand?"

"I'm happy that you don't have to. I'm happy that this is the only world you'll ever know. I'm happy that you never saw what the old world was like."

Her attention was suddenly distracted by a butterfly that floated past and she said simply, "I don't miss things like everyone else."

As her innocence floated along with the orange wings and they both walked down the hill of tall grass, toward the small cottage where Morgan stood in the doorway waiting for them, Alex spoke softly to himself.

"I don't miss things, either."

The End

AFTER LIFE

JARON LEE KNUTH

ABOUT THE AUTHOR

Jaron Lee Knuth was born in 1978. He lives in western Wisconsin.

Made in the USA
Lexington, KY
19 February 2010